C000090307

On the Verge

JANET ELLIS

The right of Janet Ellis to be identified as the Author of the Work has been asserted by her in accordance with the Copyright, Designs and Patents Act 1988

All rights reserved. No part of this publication may be reproduced, stored in a retrieval system or transmitted, in any form or by any means without the prior written permission of the author, nor be otherwise circulated in any form of binding or cover other than that in which it is printed and without a similar condition being imposed on the subsequent purchaser.

All profits from the sale of 'On the Verge' will be donated to charities of the author's choice.

Published November 2015
Clifftop Publishing
www.clifftoppublishing.com

Copyright © 2015 Janet Ellis

ISBN: 978-0-9934139-2-6

Cover photograph (view from the back of Polly's house)
Copyright © Janet Ellis

For all those looking for a better
way of life

*With thanks to my Dad and
daughter-in-law Nicola
for reading the draft of On the Verge
and highlighting my mistakes,
as well as to my husband Peter for being
a critical and constructive editor.*

ACKNOWLEDGEMENTS

'Rosie' written by Don Partridge
'What is Life?' written by George Harrison
Free Clipart used on map
Various websites which provided:-
    Sunrise and sunset times in Greece
    School term times in Greece
    Calendar for 2002

ALSO BY THE AUTHOR

Timotheus Pserimos Puss
The 3R's – Recipes, Reflections and Reminiscences

INTRODUCTION

I arrived on the Greek Island of Aspros at the beginning of May 2002. Before I left the UK, I promised myself I would keep a diary; recording my time away. It was my intention not to leave this as random jottings in notebooks. On my return, I would collate and turn these into a story format which I suppose in some ways could be termed, my memoirs.

That was over eleven years ago and since then I have made excuses, finding other more pressing things to do or I have just conveniently forgotten. But every time I open the desk drawer and see those ragged notebooks that have been stuffed in my rucksack or rolled up before I thrust them into a pocket; I feel a nagging guilt. Guilt brought about by this broken promise. I have always been the sort of person who; if I say I am going to do something, then I do it. So over the years this broken promise has not rested easy with me.

October 2013, I decided it was time to make a start and after six weeks of considerable determination and resolve I have finished! Initially I had trepidations but I have so enjoyed working my way through the notebooks, reliving virtually every day. What was supposed to be straightforward; a five month sabbatical to be spent chilling out and doing nothing, turned into a whole lot more. But if I say too much here, I will spoil the story of how life evolved for me and how this chapter in my life has changed me into the person I am today.

I am not a writer and my grammar has never been brilliant. With this in mind, hopefully readers will tolerate my style and in particular the number of times I have written 'I this' and 'I that'. In other words my rather excessive use of 'I'!

Polly, December 2013

Village of Lionas

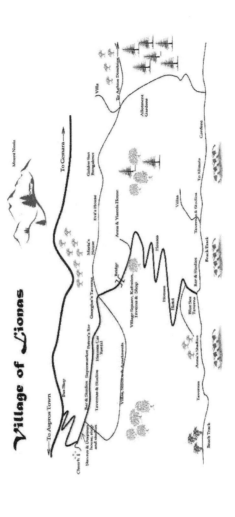

Chapter One

It was the 1st May 2002 and I had just pulled out the cases from underneath the bed when the flat's entry intercom buzzed.

"Who the heck can that be", I remember mumbling to myself as I made my way to the door. Pressing the speaker my abrupt response was "Yes!"

Downstairs Amy replied gingerly "Sorry Polly; didn't mean to disturb you. Just wondered if you needed any help?"

The honest answer was "No, go away." This was going to be difficult enough, without anyone peering over my shoulder, making what they considered to be helpful suggestions as to what I should or should not take; either as their idea of a necessity or what they felt may come in handy. But as it was Amy, how could I say "No" when it was Amy who had been my rock and who with a young family and husband had still managed to find time for me. Instead I heard myself saying cheerily "Come on up Amy."

With a forced smile, I opened the flat's door.

"Hi" greeted Amy, shortly followed with "Don't want to be intrusive. I just wondered if you needed a hand. Just taken the kids to school, I am up to date with the cleaning, ironing and gardening and Alan's mum is doing the school run this afternoon and taking them to (she screwed her face in disapproval) McDonalds for tea. So you see I don't have to go or be anywhere today." Amy shrugged her shoulders, in a gesture that said – it's up to you.

Amy had obviously planned this free time. How could I send her off home; instead I extended my smile and told a lie.

"Yes actually, I was wondering if I would get it all sorted today. I'd love some help."

Amy was, as ever, fantastic. I had already collected all my personal ornaments and pictures and placed these on the dining room table alongside a pile of newspapers. As soon as she spotted these and the stout cardboard boxes on the floor she set to wrapping each item separately and packing them carefully in the boxes. I left her to it and returned to the cases, opening them up and taking out the roll bags and rucksacks. I put them all on the floor and then started in earnest with the wardrobes, then the cupboards, followed by the drawers and by the time I had sorted my clothes and footwear into a pile to store, a pile for the charity shop and on the bed the smallest pile; the things I would take, Amy had finished in the dining room and came in with two mugs of coffee. "Time for a break." she announced. Amy spent the rest of the morning filling the suitcases with clothes and shoes to store and black plastic sacks with items for the charity shop, while I concentrated on splitting the items I was going to take between a roll bag and a rucksack. I was determined to travel light.

All finished, I sat on the bed and stared at the blank wall ahead of me. Yes, it was what the 'doctor ordered' but was this the right thing to be doing? Did I really need to go? Amy must have read my mind and brought me back from my musings with,

"Right; it's time for some lunch. What do you say we get a bit of fresh air and walk along to the Italian down the road? We can drop these sacks off at the charity shop on our way. When we get back we can store away the boxes and cases and take it from there. By the way you did keep out some clean knickers for tomorrow, didn't you?"

I couldn't help but smile.

The following morning, I sat in the lounge running through my packing list, double checking I had my passport, credit and debit cards, phone etc. Harry looked down on me, handsome as ever; tall, slightly muscular, with his dark hair brushed back.

He smiled and said softly "Ready?"

I nodded a yes and asked, "Is Mike here?"

"Yes he's downstairs waiting by the car." he replied.

It would have been all too easy to have changed my mind and stayed but I knew in my deep inner self that this was not going to achieve anything, in fact, as my doctor had warned me - it would be positively detrimental to my health. Instead I stood up positively saying,

"Okay, let's go. No looking back, Aspros here I come!"

The journey passed smoothly, no traffic problems driving to the airport, swift baggage check-in and then straight through passport control. As I walked towards the security checks, I turned to watch Harry and Mike walk back across the concourse. I saw them smile at each other while Harry's hand briefly touched Mike's. I felt a slight pang of envy as I remembered the first time Harry touched me and how it had sent a tingle throughout my body. That is in the past I told myself. I am going away. They will have time together while I give myself time to try to recover, reflect and maybe even rediscover myself.

Chapter Two

Why is it when I fly I always seem to get sat next to the 'fat man', who wedges himself into the seat, has trouble fastening his seat belt, insists on having the blowers in the overhead console going full pelt and when it comes to dropping down the tray for the inflight meal – well just forget it! No change, except today it is a woman who I am very kindly referring to here as being 'of over ample proportions'. Still never mind, I had managed before - Get on with it Polly, I told myself. I settled as comfortably as you can into the space afforded to passengers on a charter flight and started the first stage of my self-prescribed therapy; reflecting on all the things that had happened over the past five or so years, which had made me depressed and driven me to the point of being on the verge of a nervous breakdown (my doctors words, not mine). On more than one occasion I struggled to hold back floods of tears. A couple of times one of the flight attendants stopped and asked if everything was okay. I assured them I was fine. Three hours into the flight, at the point when I could feel we were starting the descent, I was back in control and starting to think what I needed to do after the plane had landed.

My feelings now were those of both nervousness and anticipation; I was about to start a five month sabbatical on the small Greek island of Aspros, on my own and away from friends, colleagues and family.

We landed with the usual thump, as the pilot put the plane down on the island's short runway and almost immediately put the engines into reverse thrust. If he got it wrong, none of them ever did, we would disappear off the end of the tarmac and plunge into the sea. Safely down, a short taxi to the terminal, engines off and the doors opened ready for disembarking. I paused at the top of the steps for a few seconds, long enough to allow the balminess of an Asprian spring day to pass over me before descending and walking to the terminal. Here, there was all the usual chaos at baggage reclaim. I quickly sent a text to Amy, Harry and the office which simply said "Arrived! Sun is shining and it's warm!" Shortly after, my roll bag came up on the carousel and with my rucksack on my back, I proceeded out into the main concourse, through the melee of tourists and travel reps and on towards the exit. I strode with confidence towards the doors, blocking out the general hubbub and it was not until I was just about to walk outside that I was aware someone was calling my name, "Polleee!" As I turned, a breathless man stood in front of me, a man I recognised immediately. It was Yiannis, looking a little more rounded and with less hair than when I last saw him but his characteristic cheeky smile was just the same.

"Thought I wasn't going to catch up with you." he gasped, before extending his smile still further and saying "Want a lift?"

He had taken me by surprise and I uttered an inadequate response "Well yes, yes please. I really wasn't expecting anyone."

"Oh, I was on my way back from town" Yiannis replied "and saw it was about the time you were due to land, so I stopped off to see if I could save you the taxi fare."

This was so kind and typical of Asprians and Greeks in general.

No surprises in the airport car park; Yiannis was still driving his old battered red van. How it held together over the rough and potholed dirt roads, I never knew and the fact it had survived since I was last on the island was indeed a testimonial to the van's manufacturer. Bags in the back, we were soon off through the countryside and twisting village lanes, bordered with whitewashed houses, before emerging on the main island road. With the van's windows open, I sat back letting Yiannis do all the talking while I savoured the different aromas; vanilla from the gorse, spices from dishes cooking in village kitchens etc. Yiannis chatted away about the children; their four boys,

Dimitri, Christos, Kostas and Spiros and of course their newest edition, who I had yet to meet, their daughter, Karis. As we motored on, I also took delight from passing familiar places, the roadside taverna in Afrata, the beginning of a footpath over to Aghios Christoforos Monastery, the old German World War II motor bike and so on. All the time I was concentrating on what Yiannis was telling me but at the same time I was supressing a growing excitement. My nervousness had gone. It felt great to be back on Aspros!

As we turned right off the main road and started descending into Lionas, the van groaned and clunked as Yiannis steered round bends of varying acute angles. While the van was vocal, Yiannis was quiet. After a while he broke his silence.

"Polly," he started "actually it was Anna who told me to go to the airport. You see, the house, Maria's house, isn't quite ready. Stavros is so embarrassed but Despina has been in hospital and when she came out there were problems, so he has been left to get the shop and the studios ready and well just hasn't had the time to sort Maria's house." He looked embarrassed and took a deep breath before continuing, "Anna said as I had made the arrangement for you to rent the house that I must pick you up from the airport so I could explain. Anna has been there this morning just to make sure it is fit to sleep in and you will eat with our family this evening."

He sighed and waited to hear what my reaction would be. Although I was annoyed, this was not the time to show it, after all it was nobody's fault. I assured Yiannis that I was sure everything would be fine and yes I would love to join the family in the evening. By then we had reached the turning on the left just after Georgios's taverna and we bumped our way up the dirt track some 200 metres or so and there on the left stood Maria's house.

It was as I remembered it when I first walked past with Amy (before she married Alan) and then a few years later with Harry as we made our way to the ruined monastery of Aghios Dimitrios. The house is best described as a bungalow and had been the home of Stavros's mother Maria; until she was taken ill and died during the previous winter. It was typical of the island's houses; a red tile roof with white painted walls and green shutters. From the metal gate, there was a concrete path leading to a covered veranda with vines growing over, providing shade in the summer months. The garden was somewhat overgrown and the whole plot was bordered with a rendered wall, once painted white, now cracking and flaking, with weeds taking advantage of the resulting nooks and crannies.

Yiannis took my bag and rucksack out of the van, while I stood by the gate.

"Is it as you remember?" he asked.

"Oh yes, definitely" I replied "Can we go in, I have never been inside."

Yiannis took the house keys out of his pocket and handed them to me, gesturing me to go ahead. Following behind, he put my bags down on the veranda by the door. Walking back towards his van he called,

"I'll come back and pick you up about eight then. Oh, I nearly forgot; the mattress, it is brand new."

I was pleased he was not going to hang around but I declined the offer of the lift. I knew where they lived and wanted to walk down through the village on my own and savour the sounds and smells of the island's evening.

After what Yiannis had said, I was not sure what to expect when I turned the key in the door and walked inside Maria's house. It smelt a little musty and with only shafts of sun light filtering through the closed shutters, there was little I could see. This was soon remedied and with all the windows and shutters open, all was revealed. The front door led straight into the living area, with two windows, one to the front, the other to the side. To the right an archway led into the kitchen area with a window looking over the front garden and a door leading out to the side. At the back of the living area a door led into an inner lobby with a large built-in cupboard on the back wall. To the left was a bedroom with windows to the side and back and to the right, a sliding door into the bathroom and further up the lobby another door leading into another bedroom, again with a window to the side and another to the back. The furnishings were all typical dark wood and traditional, there were mats on the tiled floors, both the beds had new mattresses and Anna, bless her, had made up the bed in the bedroom next to the bathroom with brightly coloured new linen. The bathroom had probably been refitted in the past few years and joy of joys, it had a washing machine! From the smell of bleach I could tell Anna had been busy in here and she had left a pile of new towels on the shelf. The kitchen was basic with a cooker, fridge-freezer, rudimentary units and wall racks. Of all the rooms, it was the kitchen that was most in need of attention.

There was a note on the kitchen table, under a tin of coffee, saying, 'Welcome Polly. A few essentials in the fridge. See you later. Anna'. I opened the fridge and had to laugh at Anna's idea of a 'few essentials'; a container of milk, a packet of biscuits and a bottle of retsina wine. I looked at my watch, goodness it was 6 o'clock already. I should have realised, as the sun was starting to drop and the light was starting to fade. Right Polly, I thought, time for a shower, clean set of clothes and then I will have enough time to sit out on the veranda with a glass of wine before walking down through the village to Yiannis's and Anna's house. In early May the evenings still have a chill to them but this did not detract from the pleasure I experienced sat outside sipping that glass of wine and munching a few biscuits, while I looked through the tall columnar cypress trees on the opposite side of the track and down towards the sea.

I left Maria's house with plenty of time to slowly meander down through the village and up to Yiannis's and Anna's. At the end of the track, I turned left to join the main village road and saw that Georgios already had a few diners. As this was the beginning of the tourist season they too had probably flown in today. I reflected on my first visit to Aspros. It was also my first visit to Greece and along with Amy, we were not sure what to expect. As it was, each day we grew to love and appreciate the island more until at the end of our two weeks holiday, we didn't want to go home. On the last day we fantasized and giggled about us falling in love with Greek men, marrying and staying here forever. Looking back, it showed how immature we were, but then, what harm can a bit of fantasizing do?

Walking over the bridge, I could not resist looking down into the ravine. Mmm, no changes, full of old defunct battered washing machines, fridges, freezers and the like. This was something I could never understand about the Greeks. They live in such wonderful unspoilt surroundings and yet they blot areas like these with their cast-offs. Still it's their country and it is not my place to criticise how they treat it; well not too strongly anyway. A few more bends, passing holiday villas and local houses and I was in the village with its taverna, kafenion and small shop. It was so small there was no village square as such but on the right, to the side of the kafenion and shop, there was an area with a huge plane tree where chairs and tables were grouped under its vast boughs. To the side a small stream gurgled its way down to the communal washing area. This was no longer used by the village women; housewives had long since converted to labour saving washing machines. A few old men were sat under the plane tree playing tavli, some with a glass of ouzo, and others with a coffee.

"Καλησπέρα σας" "Good evening" they called as I passed.

In return I replied, "Και σε σας ένα καλό βράδυ." "And to you a good evening."

The taverna was on the left and just after this I took the steep turning that would lead me to Yiannis's and Anna's.

As I approached their white modern rendered two storey flat roofed house, the door was open and I could hear the sound of talking from inside.

I knocked on the door and walked slowly in calling "Γεια σας, είμαι εδώ." "Hello, I am here."

Anna greeted me as she came across the hall from the kitchen and hugged me.

"So good to see you Polly." she said in her American Greek accent. "Come in, we are all in the kitchen. Well nearly all of us, the two youngest have gone to bed but you will see them of course another day."

I thanked her for the cleaning she had done, as well as the new linen and towels. She insisted it was nothing and it was her pleasure to help. In the kitchen Yiannis was stood next to the table and by his side were Dimitri, Christos and Kostas. Needless to say all three boys had grown since I last saw them but they still retained recognisable features. Dimitri was now 13 and like his dad; you could tell just by looking at his face he was a rebel. Christos was 11, slim in the face with light brown hair like his mum and Kostas who was 9 now wore glasses, giving him a studious look. Greetings exchanged and with a glass of wine in my hand we went outside where Yiannis barbequed souvlaki. Anna and I sat down at the large wooden table; she sat back in her chair with a sigh. She explained she had had a busy day and was happy for Yiannis to take over the cooking. She had been called into school because of Dimitri's disruptive behaviour, then there was the washing, shopping and just enough time to have a quick clean at Maria's house before she picked up the boys from school. She then had to prepare the evening meal, cook for six year old Spiros and two year old Karis, put them to bed which as usual they went to, grudgingly. She took a sip from her glass of wine, "Boy, there are times when I could really do with two pairs of hands!" she smiled.

Then came the inevitable question, why was I here on my own, where was Harry and why had I come for five months? I really was not prepared to go into details, maybe at a later date but not now. I managed to skirt around the questions, telling Anna that Harry would be coming out in July and told a fib that things were quiet at work and I had decided to take time off until business picked up. I could see she was not convinced but she obviously appreciated this was not the time to probe further.

What followed was an enjoyable evening with us all sat chatting round the large wooden table, eating tasty souvlaki, salads dressed with olive oil and wonderful local bread. I was thankful that Anna being a Greek American and Yiannis who had spent time in the United States, where he met Anna, both had a good command of English. The boys were learning English at school so I did not have to use my limited Greek too often. As I did not have a great grasp of tenses, conjugating verbs and grammar in general, this led the boys to fall about laughing, when what I was trying to say, came out as total nonsense. I told them, I had five months to improve and that from now on they should only speak to me in Greek. This went down like a lead balloon as they wanted to practice their English on me, so we compromised; they would talk to me in English, I would answer in Greek and we would both correct the others mistakes. I wasn't sure if this would work but the theory was sound enough.

We chatted on long after we had finished eating. It was just after 11 o'clock when I hit a brick wall. I completely ran out of oomph; I had been up since five that morning, not a strenuous day sitting on a plane, being driven to Maria's house etc. but tiring all the same. Anna took one look in my direction and said,

"I think it is time we all went to bed, school for you three tomorrow but first I want you Dimitri to take Anna back on the scooter."

Well if anything brought me back to my senses it was the thought of sitting pillion behind a thirteen year old. Seeing my shock, Anna added,

"Dimitri is a very cautious driver. Dimitri wants to start driving his father's van and he can't do that until he proves he can handle the scooter in a proper manner. Can you Dimitri?"

His response was in his best English, "You know I can handle the scooter mum, I will take good care, Polly has nothing to worry about."

But I could see by the look on his face, if I had been one of his mates; I would have been in for a white knuckle ride. I did wonder if Dimitri should be driving at thirteen but there are lots of rules and regulations that are ignored on this small Greek island. An island so low in crime it boasts just one police officer.

I said my farewells and despite my insistence that I would be all right, Anna maintained she would stop by tomorrow. I climbed on the scooter behind Dimitri who told me to put my arms round his waist and as we disappeared from the view of his parents he said,

"Hold on tight!"

This was his little joke because he rode the scooter with caution, avoiding potholes; I had a very sedate journey back.

As I dismounted he asked "Good wasn't I? Please, you will tell mum tomorrow, I was good?"

"Of course." I replied.
I smiled to confirm and with that he turned the scooter round and headed off hell for leather down the track leaving a trail of dust behind him. I had to laugh.

I walked up the path onto the veranda and turned the key in the lock. As I opened the door, I contemplated whether to have one more glass of wine or go straight to bed. It was the wine that won. Yes, I was totally bushed but I would sit out on the veranda with a chilled glass of retsina, unwind and look up at the stars.

Chapter Three

May 3rd, my first complete day and I woke to the sound of banging on the door and a man's voice shouting,

"Pollee, Pollee"

I came quickly to my senses and looked at my watch. It was 9 o'clock. Oh my goodness, I had slept well. A man, quick, I can't go to the door in my nightwear. I grabbed my fleece, rammed my arms down the sleeves and zipped it up while at the same time I headed for the door shouting,

"Εδώ είμαι εδώ." "Here, I'm here."

I opened the door and stood on the veranda and instantly recognisable was Stavros. I beckoned him in; he looked me up and down, was a little hesitant given my state of dress or lack of state of dress but came in, leaving the door open behind him. He burst forth with a torrent of apologies about the house not being ready, the state of the garden, how ill Despina had been and how he had to get the shop and studios ready to open on his own. When he talked about his beloved wife Despina I could see tears in his eyes. Yes, he had promised the house would be cleaned, aired and ready for my arrival but how could I be cross with a man who had lost his mother and whose wife had been so unwell. None of it was his fault, so I told him as best I could in a mixture of Greek and English; that it was not a problem, I had a clean bed, the shower had hot water, the toilet worked but then I hesitated. I pointed through the arch into the kitchen and shook my head,

"Όχι καλά." "Not good." I said quietly so as not to distress him.

We went through and using hand actions, I indicated it needed painting. I managed to convey that if Stavros could supply the paint and brushes, I would tackle the job. With no decorating skills, I wasn't sure why I suggested this and was relieved when Stavros told me no; decorating was not women's work; he would come tomorrow and do the job. That was all very well but what about his shop. I asked if Despina was well enough to run the shop. He shrugged his shoulders, she would manage, it was only if someone wanted an item off a high shelf that there would be a problem, she would just have to ask them to come back another time. I don't know why but I found myself offering to sit with Despina in the shop, so I could help if needed. I had never met Despina; she had either been in the house or cleaning the studios but never in the shop when I came in search of unusual gifts to take home. Stavros smiled in appreciation and we arranged that he would come along around 8 o'clock the following morning and start painting and then later I would walk up to the shop to be there in time for when Despina would open it at ten.

Stavros went off immediately to town to buy the paint, leaving me to get dressed and eat a breakfast of coffee and biscuits. I sat out on the veranda and started on a list of 'things to do'. I always found lists made tasks seem less daunting and of course there was the satisfaction of ticking off each task after I had completed it. Cleaning was something I had not done for quite a few years. Harry and I employed a cleaner who came to the flat twice a week and not only kept everything pristine but did the ironing too. She was an absolute treasure but here in Aspros, it would be down to me to dust, mop, wash and iron. No point sitting there thinking about what needed to be done, I started straight away by giving my bedroom a good clean; getting down the cobwebs, washing the paint work, brushing out the wardrobe, dusting inside the chest of drawers, washing the floor and beating the two rugs but the first task was to take down the curtains and put them in the washing machine. If I could get them on the line before midday, they would be dry and ready to iron and hang up before I went to bed. There was plenty of washing powder and cleaning products in the kitchen but I would need to go to the shop to get some food – can't live forever on biscuits, coffee and wine!

Although the back garden was like the front, overgrown, there was a path from the kitchen door to a washing line that stretched the length of the garden. I was making good headway and had just finished pegging out the curtains when Anna popped round. It was just before midday when she walked in and rolled up her sleeves ready to give a hand. "The kitchen is pretty grim." she remarked.

So I told her about Stavros's visit and assured her I was happy to tackle the rest on my own. It was a good way to get to know Maria's house; already I was warming to her little home that was to be my home for the next five months. Anna asked about the scooter ride home the previous evening.

"Perfect" I replied. "Look no grey hairs." Anna laughed. "But changing the subject, the new linen and towels, how much do I owe you Anna?"

"Oh nothing, when I offered to clean the bedroom and bathroom, Stavros asked me if I had any new sheets and towels because what with Despina not being well, she has not replenished stocks for their studios. Well of course I always have supplies in case I need to replace those at our beach studios. So Stavros will pay Yiannis next time he sees him. No problem. Well, if I really cannot be of help, I will go and collect Karis; she has been playing with a friend all morning. I'll pop in from time to time, if that is Okay?" she concluded. "Yes, great, the kitchen will soon be sorted, so next time I'll be able to offer you a coffee!"

It was one thirty before I realised how hungry I was. I had just finished washing the floor, so it was a good time to take a break. I decided I would eat lunch at Georgios's and then rather than walking down to the village, I would shop at the tourist supermarket a bit further up the road. I brushed my hair, slapped on some lipstick so that I looked halfway respectable (it seemed pointless getting cleaned up as I still had the carpets to beat), before taking the short walk up the dirt track and into Georgios's taverna. I thought I would be able to slip in and sit at a table overlooking the garden but Georgios spotted me and as he does to everyone, asked in Greek how I was. Of course, you were expected to reply in Greek and if you didn't, he would supply you with the right phrase and expect you to remember this when you next came into eat. He never forgot a face. I was prepared and replied, I was very well, I asked him how he was and then for a table next to the garden. Georgios was delighted; he asked if I had been studying the Greek language. I was able to tell him; yes, I had had lessons but then I let myself down a bit by using the present tense. He asked me if I liked small fish as he had gavros delivered fresh that morning. I had planned to have a Greek salad with a bottle of water to drink but how could I refuse a plate of fresh fish. So I ordered gavros and decided, ένα τέταρτο λίτρο, a quarter litre of house wine was far more fitting an accompaniment than water. I started writing a shopping list and after about ten minutes Georgios brought out the freshly fried fish topped with a wedge of lemon, as well as a small lettuce salad, a chunk of village bread and my wine. Everything was perfect; I had almost forgotten how good these little fishes tasted. When I had finished, the taverna was empty and I went inside in search of Georgios to pay. Georgios asked where I was staying and for how long. Expecting me to say either one or two weeks, he was a little surprised when I said, five months. He looked into my eyes and said sincerely,

"If you ever need help, you come and see me. You understand?"

I understood; a woman living on her own in an area frequented by tourists may possibly need assistance. After thanking him I walked up the hill to the supermarket. I kept my shopping to the minimum; with the cupboards to clean after Stavros had finished painting, it made sense not to buy too much. I settled for the ingredients to make a Greek salad for my supper, a loaf of bread, cereal, bottled water, orange squash, toilet paper and some factor 15 sun lotion. That would be enough for now.

Back at Maria's house, I took the curtains off the line and folded them ready to iron and then beat the bedroom rugs; it's amazing how dust accumulates even when a house is empty. With the rugs back on the floor and the curtains ironed and rehung, I emptied the contents of my roll bag and rucksack onto the bed. Two pairs of shorts, four t-shirts, a pair of jeans, two lightweight fleeces, underwear, walking socks, swimsuit, flip flops, sandals, a pair of summer shoes, handbag and the all essential 'posh frock'. These along with the clothes I travelled in and those I was wearing now, were the total sum of my wardrobe. I had also brought a few essential toiletries, my make-up, supply of my prescription tablets, camera, mp3 player, torch, Dictaphone, two plug adaptors, dictionary (English/Greek), pens, pencils and a decent sized note book. Not much for five months but I wanted to live simply; free of clutter.

With my meagre selection of clothes stowed away in the wardrobe and chest of drawers, it was time for a shower. Feeling suitably refreshed I decided supper would have to wait. First I would take a walk up the dirt track to see if anything had changed. I tied a fleece round my waist, put my torch and mobile phone in the pocket of my jeans and set off. Maria's house was not exactly what you would call isolated but there's a reasonable distance before the next dwelling. The house was of a similar style to Maria's, although it had to be said, the garden was in far better upkeep. Without wanting to appear too nosey, I looked to see what was growing in the front garden; this would give me a good idea as to which plants flourished in the local soil. Most popular were roses and I was surprised as to how disease free they were. Amy was always complaining about how hers suffered from greenfly, blackfly, blackspot, mildew and the like, to the point when she threatened to dig them all out. There was no grass, just weed free brown earth surrounding them with the occasional group of marigolds giving colour closer to ground level. Geraniums in pots of assorted shapes and sizes featured on the veranda and a variety of trailing vines including bougainvillea and grapes scrambled over the top.

I continued on and was somewhat alarmed to see ahead of me and set back from the track, a group of around twenty holiday bungalows. I was alarmed because of their gaudy bright colours and there was nothing that you could describe as traditional about them, apart from shutters at the windows. I was concerned as to what sort of tourists these would attract. As I drew closer I could see the development was called Χρυσός Ήλιος, Golden Sun. Some bungalows still had their shutters closed; as it was the first week of the season there was bound to be under occupancy. But looking towards those with open shutters, I could see couples sat on their patios either reading or playing cards; they all had glasses and bottles on their patio tables. Some had come with friends and were sharing a patio, chatting and laughing as they sipped from their glasses. So long as the season carried on as it had started and with fingers crossed there were no rowdy parties, then this small complex should not pose a problem.

After about twenty minutes I came to the junction where the track to the left takes you up to a large villa and straight on continues to the ruined monastery of Aghios Dimitrios. I chose the track to the right, leading to, what we would call in the UK, allotments. I walked down a short way to have a peek at what was being grown; again looking for ideas, this time as to what to plant at the back of Maria's house. There was no shortage of water in this area and in the fading light I could see old men carrying cans and buckets of water towards their crops. I decided I had gone far enough and retraced my steps back to Maria's house. Most of the Golden Sun bungalows were deserted; no doubt their occupants had gone to one of the village tavernas for dinner.

I prepared my salad using the cucumber, green pepper, red onion and a huge red tomato, I had bought earlier. This was topped with a good chunk of feta cheese and finally olive oil poured over. But two things were missing; I had forgotten to buy olives and oregano. Oh well, I would have to go without. I cut a chunk of bread and took this with my salad, olive oil, wine glass and the rest of yesterday's bottle of retsina, out onto the veranda. By then the light had faded and I needed to turn on the small overhead light to see what I was eating. I had forgotten just how intense the flavours of Greek salad vegetables are; full of the sun that had encouraged their growth and in the case of tomatoes, that had ripened them too. The bread was delicious dipped in olive oil and then in the juices at the bottom of my bowl of salad. Supper finished I sat back with the wine and my notebook and pen. Goodness, I had only been here for just over a day and yet there was so much to log. I had really expected to be writing about a day relaxing on the beach and not about cleaning and shopping! The next hour or so was spent scribbling and sipping until everything was noted, from Amy's arrival at the flat up to today's salad supper. By then I had drunk the bottle of retsina dry and was feeling mellow. After exchanging "Good Nights" with the tourists who were returning to their holiday bungalows, I decided it was time for me to hit the sack.

Chapter Four

May 4th; day two and I woke about 6 a.m. After a hasty breakfast, I cleared the kitchen of moveable items ready for Stavros's arrival. This was followed by taking down the curtains in the spare bedroom and putting them in the washing machine. The curtains were pegged out on the line before Stavros arrived with pots of paint, brushes and a ladder but I noted; no dust sheets. He was keen to make a start, so I promised to keep out of his way until it was time to walk up to the shop. Armed with a bucket of soapy water and some rags I disappeared outside to clean the windows. Around 9.30 a.m. and with the windows shiny and clean, it was time to go indoors for a quick change into something more presentable. Before I left to walk up to the shop, I stuck my head through the arch, where Stavros was up the ladder painting the ceiling, and shouted goodbye. I didn't dare look at the floor to see if any paint had dripped from the brush onto the tiles!

Making my way up the track, I called "Καλημέρα." "Good morning." to Georgios and then turned up the tarmac road towards the main tourist part of the village. There was little change here, apart from a couple of new blocks of studios. I had just passed the car hire office when Anna, driving a grey 4x4, in better nick than the red van but only just, pulled up alongside.

"Off to Despina's?" she enquired through the open passenger window.

"Yes, I am." I replied.

"Jump in." she instructed as she stretched across to open the door.

Well it was only about another couple of hundred metres from the shop but I accepted the lift all the same.

"You need to know'" Anna started, "Despina is not only recovering from surgery but there are mental issues she is trying to come to terms with too. She had a hysterectomy which is one thing but of course any hopes they may have had of having a family has gone out of the window. She's in her mid-40's now but I think she still hoped that one day she would be able to tell Stavros that she was pregnant. So she blames herself that they have no children and this along with the change in hormone levels makes her depressed, hence the mental issues. No matter how many times we tell her and Stavros does too, that this is what God intended and it is not her fault, she still reproaches herself."

Anna turned her head briefly towards me as she pulled up outside the shop and I nodded sympathetically saying,

"I understand Anna, don't worry, I will tread carefully."

Anna pulled away and I stood at the edge of the road thinking to myself; yes I understand only too well what Despina is going through, nobody can help you except yourself. There had been nights and there would probably be more, when I would cry myself to sleep, thinking of what can never be.

I went down the three steps to the shop door and opened it calling to Despina to let her know I had arrived. She came shuffling through the door at the back of the shop; she winced and pointed to her abdomen. Yes, I thought, very sore from the incision. Her face was grey and her greasy brown hair was pulled back and tied with a rubber band. She wore a loose blue patterned dress, a pair of flip flops and no jewellery, apart from her wedding ring. What a sight, enough to frighten away anyone who came into the shop. Her appearance was probably another reason why Stavros was hesitant about leaving her alone in the shop. With my limited vocabulary I could only motion to her to sit down on the stool behind the counter. I looked round the shop at the stock on the shelves and hanging on rails. Well Despina may look like a wreck but she certainly had an eye for attractive gifts; I could not imagine a man would make such selections. I turned to Despina, smiled my approval saying,

"Πολύ καλά" "Very good."

Despina smiled and within that smile I could see a beauty that was being stifled by her sorrow.

The morning soon passed with us communicating mainly through gestures and signs. A few tourists came into the shop, none of them left without buying something and we sold two sundresses, a pair of sunglasses, a key ring and a necklace. Despina was well pleased and when she heard my stomach rumbling, she shuffled through the back of the shop, returning with a glass of lemonade, a dish of meatballs in tomato sauce and a thick slice of bread. I sat on the chair outside to eat; a chair where men, who did not want to indulge in shopping, could sit and wait for their wives, girlfriends, daughters etc. Rather a strange arrangement but I was sure Despina had her reasons for not wanting me to eat in their private area at the back and with an outside loo, I suppose there was no reason for me to go inside their house. The meatballs were delicious, made from lamb and flavoured with cinnamon and I could tell the sauce was made with fresh tomatoes and not tinned.

"Absolutely delicious." I told Despina and even though she understood very little English, my face obviously conveyed what I could not say in Greek.

In the afternoon we took delivery of a large brown box containing more stock. Fortunately the driver carried the box down the steps and into the shop; otherwise I am sure we would have ended up unloading the contents on the roadside. Certainly Despina wouldn't have been able to help me carry such a large package. We spent the rest of the afternoon unpacking an assortment of glass and pottery items and finding places to display them on the shelves. This was in-between serving customers who carefully squeezed past the box that was taking up most of the central floor space in the shop. All done by 5 o'clock when paint splattered Stavros arrived. He couldn't see the paint in his hair and on his face. I nudged Despina and we both laughed while Stavros looked on puzzled. Stavros explained that he had not finished, that I could not use the kitchen to cook tonight and that well, he had left a mess but that he would clean it all up when he had finished. Really, I thought. According to my logic, if painting was man's work then cleaning was what women did afterwards! Stavros told me he would run me back, I refused as I had some shopping to do at the supermarket and Despina would need him now in the shop. Stavros walked out with me, he touched my shoulder, "She laughed Polly; when you nudged her, she laughed. This is the first time in weeks I have seen my Despina laugh. Maybe now she is feeling better." Yes, maybe, I thought to myself but she has a long way to go yet. We arranged that Stavros would arrive at Maria's house at the same time tomorrow when he hoped to finish painting the kitchen.

I walked back, stopping at the supermarket for a few essentials, which included an all-important bottle of wine plus a jar of olives and a bag of oregano for the larder cupboard. It was a glorious late afternoon and walking back up the track to Maria's house, I enjoyed feeling the sun on my face. While I was walking along the track I remembered the curtains on the line. They would be absolutely bone dry and I would have to damp them down before I could iron them. I hoped that the sun had not started to fade them, if they had that would be so embarrassing; I could see they were quite new. I dumped my shopping on the veranda and went round the back to unpeg the curtains but they had gone. These days it only took the slightest thing to upset me and with the curtains no longer on the line, I panicked. Surely nobody would steal them but where had they gone? Unlocking and opening the front door; the smell of paint hit me. I quickly opened all the shutters and windows and there in the spare bedroom were the curtains, neatly laid out on top of the new mattress. Was I impressed! Stavros must have brought them in; how thoughtful and for me my panic was now over.

The kitchen was not as messy as I imagined. Just a few odd spots of paint here and there on the floor. It looked as though Stavros must have cleaned up any drips as he went along but he was right; I would not be able to cook tonight. With the strong smell of paint I decided to put the perishables, wine and water in the fridge and leave the other shopping in the living room. I was still quite full from Despina's meatballs but I would need something to eat later; I would probably go back to Georgios's for something light. He never minded if you only wanted a small amount to eat, yes it was better for him if you ordered a number of dishes but it seemed if you were happy then so was Georgios. Just enough time to iron the curtains, before taking a shower and then relaxing on the veranda, where I would write my diary for the day, accompanied by a glass of white wine.

I had just finished my diary and was sitting back enjoying the evening and the view of the sea between the cypress trees when from inside the house I heard my mobile phone ringing. It was an apologetic Amy.

"I know I promised I wouldn't phone you too soon but I have been thinking of you; down on the beach, in the sea and generally lazing around.   And well as you can imagine I am envious, so I thought I would give you a call and hear all about it and make myself feel really green! Oh and there is another reason but first tell me all."

So I told Amy all. She was horrified and gave me a lecture about how I was there to do nothing, get away from it all and how I should have insisted that someone cleaned the house and sorted the garden, instead of which I was cleaning, washing and worse of all working in a shop! I knew everything Amy said was right but I assured her I was enjoying myself and there was plenty of time to go to the beach. Amy was not entirely convinced but what could she do; nothing really as I was here on Aspros and she was there in Berkshire. To try to steer the conversation in a different direction, I asked her what was the other reason for her call. She started by going round the houses, about it being her 35th birthday at the end of May and how the family were all going out for lunch and that her mum had wanted to give her a special treat which was; the airfare from Gatwick to Aspros. I was somewhat taken aback on two counts. Firstly, that Amy's mum should be paying for her to come and see me. Ever since the first time I went back to Amy's house after school, I knew her mum disapproved of our friendship. I thought she would have relished having me out of her daughter's hair for five months. Secondly, I was supposed to be here on my own with just one visit from Harry and Mike in July. But what the heck, I was already going against 'what the doctor ordered'. So instead of telling Amy "No", I told her I would love her to come, which at the time I was not sure was quite the truth. The rest of the conversation was about when she would come (first week of June), where she would stay (here with me in Maria's house), how she would get from the airport (I would meet her in a taxi) and other bits of girly chitchat.

It was 9 o'clock before I walked along to eat at Georgios's. After exchanging greetings with him I sat down at a small table in the corner of the garden, away from other diners and where I could admire the roses. I was deep in thought when Georgios came over and placed a glass of ouzo, a small bowl of ice and a jug of water on the table.

"You look as though you need this." he commented. "It's with my complements. I will come back shortly and take your order."

Oh dear, had the thought of entertaining Amy for a week and the puzzlement as to why her mum was paying for her flight; made me look that troubled! After a few sips of ouzo I felt more relaxed and when Georgios returned I ordered tzatziki, a plate of courgette fritters and a glass of wine.

Chapter Five

May 5th, day three and I was up again at six. After breakfast I started work on the spare bedroom; first I cleaned the wardrobe, dressing table and bedside cabinet before washing the woodwork. Stavros arrived prompt on 8 o'clock, he was in a cheery mood, whistling whilst he opened the paint can and gathered together his brushes. Before he got started, I filled a bucket with water and took this with me along with the mop. I thanked him for taking the curtains off the line yesterday and asked if he would do the same again today as the washing machine had just finished and I was about to hang out the ones from the living room. He looked a bit puzzled at first.

"Oh that wasn't me." he said "Eva from up the track came bustling in mid-morning, curtains over her arm, mumbling about; if those curtains stayed out there much longer they would be too dry to iron. How can they be too dry, I asked myself? But I guess this is something you women understand. Anyway she laid them out on the spare bed, stuck her head through the archway, complained about the smell of paint and was off. So no doubt she will do the same again today. Bit of a nosey one that Eva. Hearts in the right place though." he added.

I had to smile and left Stavros to his painting while I washed the spare bedroom floor and hung out the curtains.

When I arrived at the shop, Despina was displaying some necklaces on a stand. As she walked across to the door to greet me she looked as though she was moving better today. More stock had arrived earlier that morning, a much smaller box than yesterdays. It was on the counter and contained jewellery; necklaces, pendants, bracelets and earrings, with about three of each design. Despina conveyed that we would display one of each; the rest would stay in the box which would be stored on top of the display cabinet in the corner. I was particularly struck with a matching set of pendant, drop earrings and bracelet with a mix of different shades of pale blue semi-precious stones set in a silver metal. I let Despina price these before I put them to one side on the counter, they would set Amy's blonde hair and blue eyes off perfectly and would make an excellent present for her birthday. Now I know it is customary not to pay the full price and you are supposed to barter prices down but in Despina's case, once she knew I wanted to buy the three pieces, she dropped the price by way too much and I had to negotiate the price upwards! In the end we were both happy and she put them in a silver coloured gift box and tied it with pink ribbon ready for me to give to Amy.

We hung some beach bags and straw hats, along with a selection of sarongs under the canopy outside the door. These caught the attention of passers-by and a number came inside to see what else Despina had for sale. With so much stock and variety of goods, the shop was an Aladdin's cave and most people walked out with an item either wrapped in colourful paper or in a bag with a map of the island printed on it. Despina was restricted to a few words in English so I was able to help customers with their choices and conversions from euro's to pounds sterling. With Greece changing to the euro the previous year a lot of the tourists were still thinking in drachma, in fact in some cases they were converting from euro's to sterling and then to drachmas, so as to make sure they were getting value for money. The day passed quickly and while I learnt some new Greek vocabulary from Despina she in turn learnt the English names for a number of items in the shop.

Just before 4 o'clock Stavros returned and announced he had finished painting but I would probably want to eat out again this evening as the prevailing smell of paint was rather strong. He asked if I could stay a little longer while he went and washed the paint off his face and hands and out of his hair. No problem. Despina followed him out of the back of the shop, returning after a few minutes. When paint-free Stavros emerged he offered me a lift back which once again I refused. He walked out with me and for a short distance down the road while he explained that Despina was embarrassed at the state their home had been reduced to during her illness and because of this, she had asked me to eat outside. She had told him how much she enjoyed my company and if at any time when I was passing, I should stop for a cup of coffee. He then went on to ask; if he had other business to attend to, would I come and help in the shop. This came as rather a bolt out of the blue but without giving his request too much thought I told him I would love to come and help; at the same time thinking, I hoped he would not ask too often. Stavros smiled and turned to walk back but before he did I broached the subject of paying the rent for Maria's house.

"Not a problem." he replied "Pay me at the end of the five months."

"Are you sure?" I asked "I am happy to pay in advance. Yiannis said it would be €275 per month which makes €1375 in total."

"Oh no" responded Stavros "I told Yiannis it would be €275 for just one month but as you wanted to rent for five months it would be €250 per month which is €1250 altogether. But as I said; pay me at the end."

I didn't argue but as I walked back I thought, I was sure Yiannis said it was €300 for one month and €275 for a long term rental and then I thought again. Maybe as Yiannis had acted as a kind of agent he had added a bit on for his time. He had always been a bit of a wheeler and dealer making a bit here and a bit there; so it would be like a commission. On this basis, I probably shouldn't have approached Stavros about payment but surely no real harm was done. €125 was not an unreasonable amount considering the time Yiannis had spent finding accommodation for me and then of course, Anna had prepared a couple of rooms ready for my arrival. I would give him this amount when I paid Stavros; before I went back home. Hey, but who's talking about going back home, I had only just arrived.

Such a glorious warm late afternoon, with a few wispy clouds passing across the blue skies; I decided to walk down to the beach and take a stroll along the sands before eating at one of the beach tavernas. Showered and tidied I took my torch and camera with me, grabbing a few photographs as I made my way down the twisting road. This took me through the village, passing houses and holiday accommodation until the road emerged directly onto the beach. Yiannis's taverna 'Blue Sea' was on the right but had yet to open its doors. I could see the chairs and tables stacked inside. The terrace area remained covered with the twigs and leaves that had blown in during the winter months. He told me on the way from the airport that he would not open until June, when more visitors arrived. The schools finished for summer holidays in mid-June and Dimitris would be able to help and maybe this year, Christos could be encouraged to give a hand too.

I walked first to the right along the dusty track, past 'Anna's Studios' and other small accommodations set back from the beach until I reached an outcrop of rocks. I stopped here and sat on a large smooth boulder, dangling my feet in the cool sea and taking in the beauty of the bay; a crescent of deep blue sea and golden sands. After about half an hour, I headed back along the sand stopping at the bar opposite the 'Blue Sea' for a refreshing beer. Couples were emerging from their studios and apartments, freshly showered and some rather red after spending too much time lying on the beach. Most were dressed in trousers, long sleeved tops and carried jackets to wear after the sun had set and temperatures dropped. Beer finished and with the light starting to fade I made my way to the ever popular 'To Klimata' taverna where Sophia and her brother Aris had been cooking traditional island dishes for visitors for the last twenty years. Most of the vegetables were sourced from the family garden to the side of the taverna. This was lovingly maintained by their father Theo and mother Ariadne. In the evenings Theo carefully watered their crops while Ariadne sat preparing vegetables for the kitchen. I chose their speciality, moussaka, which was not too oily, incorporated potatoes as well as, aubergines, minced lamb cooked in olive oil, tomato puree and cinnamon; all covered with a thin layer of sauce and topped with kefalotyri cheese. By the end of the cooking the cheese was brown and crunchy and for anyone visiting Aspros; this was a dish not to be missed.

The walk back up to Maria's house was strenuous and if you had indulged in one too many glasses of wine; it was extremely sobering. While I chose to saunter slowly down on the way back I strode up with determination and by the time I reached the junction at Georgios's taverna I could feel that my cheeks were glowing from the exertion.

I finished the day in what seemed to be becoming the norm; sipping a glass of wine on the veranda whilst, writing my diary, watching the stars and exchanging "Good Night" with the tourists returning to their bungalows at the Golden Sun. Today I took time to recap on my first three full days here in the village of Lionas and how I had found little time to dwell on what Amy referred to as 'My Problems'.

Chapter Six

From now on I will condense the days, weeks and months, as my five months on Aspros unfold.

I woke up on 'Day Four' at about 5.30 a.m. It was still dark and the air temperature cool. Instead of getting up I remained snuggled in the warm, under the sheets and blanket. I started to make a plan in my head of how to progress with the cleaning and the garden. I had never had a garden to tend before and was itching to start work clearing this spring's weed growth and to start planting vegetables. I had not really surveyed the back garden apart from when I was out pegging and unpegging the curtains. There were a couple of what I presumed were fruit trees, an overgrown vegetable patch and a stone built shed which no doubt was the home for spiders and other creepy crawlies. By the time I got up I had outlined the daily routine that I would follow until I had Maria's house and garden up to scratch. My day would start in the garden when it was cool, followed by breakfast about nine and then cleaning inside until lunch time. In the afternoon, when it was at its warmest I would either shop, take a walk or just chill out on the veranda. Once the temperatures cooled, at around 5 p.m., I would resume in the garden rounding the day off with dinner on the veranda and my usual glass of wine while I wrote my diary.

The regime worked well with deviations on some days; in particular when I walked up to the main road and took the bus into Aspros main town. It was due about 8 a.m. but if the ferry from the mainland, which docked on the opposite side of the island, was late this could result in the bus being delayed three quarters of an hour or more. Over time I became known by more locals then quite often they would stop and give me a lift but for my first few bus rides I stood and waited with the tourists. If the bus was late, the local taxi driver, Thanassis, would often take advantage of this and come cruising along the road. Those tourists who were beginning to doubt if the bus would arrive at all would frequently wave and beckon him to stop. If there were four in the party Thanassis would charge one fare but if two separate couples got in he would charge each couple separately, thus doubling his fare. Naughty really, but I suppose there was some logic in it. I enjoyed my bus rides with the passengers off the ferry; quite often looking shattered and in need of sleep and villagers picked up along the way who would be chatting away to each other nineteen to the dozen. Then there were the tourists who, if it was their first journey to town, were puzzled as to why their fare had not been collected and then became bemused when Petros, the driver, pulled off the road and turned off the engine about a mile outside of town. Safely parked, Petros made his way down the aisle collecting fares; most times he knew exactly where everyone had got on but if he forgot it was down to the honesty of the passenger. Petros refused to speak anything but Greek; so those tourists who had not learnt their numbers often just held out a handful of coins, allowing him to take the required fare. If they could not manage to say "Ευχαριστώ" "Thank you" when he handed them their ticket he would tut and shake his head in disapproval. It was part of a game Petros liked to play, to make tourists feel embarrassed that they had not made the effort to learn 'Thank you'. I never had a problem with this, I feel it is down to tourists to learn a few essential words and in my case; I built on my understanding of the Greek language each time I visited the islands. Even with lessons, I still had an awful long way to go but I hoped over the next five months my grasp of tenses and vocabulary would increase further.

Once in town I had about four hours or so before the one and only return bus set off from the station. This was a designated parking area in front of a kafenion on the outskirts of the town. There were two other buses, one going north and the other starting north before heading across the mountains to the east. All three left at the same time. Fortunately each bus was clearly marked with their destinations; so no real risk of ending up in the wrong place! Four hours in town was plenty, allowing me time to walk round the market, visit the supermarket for items not stocked in the two local shops in Lionas and a stroll down the main street, stopping for a coffee at one of the many small cafés in town. If I went on a Tuesday, in addition to the daily market, the locals brought in their excess produce for sale. Gathered from their gardens at the crack of dawn, they could not have been any fresher. Their produce was generally displayed in the back of a trailer and as they did not want to take anything back with them; there were often bargains to be had towards the end of the morning. I always checked the prices on the main stalls before approaching a local producer, just in case they tried to overcharge me. If I felt this was the case, I would politely refuse and walk away.

On my first visit to town my main aim was to buy seeds for the vegetable plot plus tomato and pepper plants to grow in pots. I found the seed merchant in a side street where there were bins containing different types of beans and peas as well as packet seeds on a stand. The shelves were stacked with all types of pesticides and insecticides and there were racks of garden implements on display. The shop had a distinctive odour about it, not unpleasant, a sort of mix of earth and manure. I did not need many bean seeds, so I chose to take a small scoop from one of the bins. I sourced the others from the pre-packed varieties, choosing just one of the flowers; marigolds. I had heard they were effective at keeping away whitefly and seen them on the allotments as well as, just up the track, in Eva's garden. Even if they didn't work, they would be quite pretty to have dotted around the garden. Gardening gloves was the final item on my list but did they sell them? I knew the name for garden 'κήπος' but I did not have the foggiest what the word for gloves was in Greek.

So instead of asking or trying to explain what I wanted by using sign language, I scanned the shelves and displays and just when I was about to resign myself to rough hands and nails caked with soil, I spotted them. Obviously not a great seller, two very dusty pairs were on a high hook. With a large number of weeds to clear in Maria's garden, I decided to take both pairs. The market had a good display of plants and after buying two tomatoes and four peppers, I just could not resist a couple of geraniums. At this point, loaded with bags, I decided it was time for a coffee on the square and to pursue the local hobby - people watching.

Although bus times on the way in were a bit hit and miss the return bus left promptly at 1.30 p.m. – not a minute earlier or later than that displayed on the kafenion's wall clock. On my first visit, I was there ready and waiting at ten past one but after this; on arrival I would set my watch by the kafenion's clock and that way I need only return five minutes before departure. I was rather pleased with my purchases and after getting off the bus and starting the walk down into the village, I stopped off to see Despina and Stavros. I was welcomed with a smile, a hug and an offer of a glass of refreshing lemonade, which I gladly accepted. Despina was looking much better, her hair was still tied back but no longer appeared greasy and she was wearing make-up and jewellery; a distinct improvement. Stavros complimented me on choosing healthy plants and suggested instead of planting the tomatoes and peppers in pots that I should put them directly into the soil and make a moat round each plant. To explain what he meant, he put one of my pepper plants on the ground and using his hands imitated pulling the soil away round the pot. He explained the soil in the pots would dry out quickly but I could flood the moat with water and this would keep the plants moist for much longer. What a good idea. He laughed as he told me, that if I did anything wrong he was sure Eva would put me right! I am sure she would; every time she passed by her eyes scrutinised whatever I was doing.

It took me another ten days to complete cleaning the house and bringing the garden back to some stage of normality. Indoors it was a case of continuing with washing down woodwork and walls and thoroughly cleaning the kitchen cupboards, their contents and the cooker. Stavros had done a good job with the painting but I kept finding the odd splash or blob of paint here and there. I took time to dust and study the framed pictures in the living room. Stavros had told me if I didn't want them on the walls, I was to take them down and store them in a cupboard. But I liked them; they were mainly photographs of groups, presumably family, one of the mountain top covered in snow and another of two men sat under the plane tree in the village square, one playing a bouzouki and the other a lyre with a bow. The latter was my favourite; those two men looked so relaxed, intent on their music and totally oblivious of the person taking the photo. I would have to ask Stavros who they were.

Outside, the brick shed yielded all I needed for the garden plus unwanted spiders as well as beetles, woodlice and the like. I managed, with the aid of a broom, to convince them to move to new quarters. I was surprised there were no families of marauding mice; all the tools, balls of string and even a few packets of old seeds had remained intact. The ground was still fairly moist and the weeds lifted easily. When Eva saw me she instructed me through gestures to leave them to dry out on the surface. I could see the logic, let the roots dry out and the weed would die, I could then either burn or compost them. Fires in the open are often frowned upon in Greece, especially in the summer months, when if they got out of hand they could devastate whole hillsides. Not a good idea; instead I constructed a composter using a hammer and nails found in the shed and odd bits of wood lying around. It certainly could not be described as a solid construction but it was the best I could do with my limited carpentry skills and the materials available.

By the end of the ten days the house smelt fresh and sweet. I loved to have the windows and shutters open and see the curtains billowing, with the breezes bringing in scented wafts from the wild herbs and flowers. With the roses in bloom, sitting on the veranda was a sheer pleasure as indeed was the back garden with its two trees, which Stavros had identified as a lemon and an almond. The trees were set towards the back wall; the shed was in one corner with the composter next to it and closer to the house was the vegetable patch. I had planted the tomatoes and peppers as Stavros suggested and next to them were lines of seed drills with areas in between sown with marigolds. All that was left was the wall at the front to sort. I felt very proud of my efforts and sad as it may sound I kept walking round the garden and then in the house with a grin of satisfaction on my face.

Chapter 7

I guess I was now worthy of a visit. A couple of days into my third week Eva arrived on the doorstep along with another lady who she introduced as Elpida. Eva presented me with a basket of musmula fruits and Elpida handed me a plate of biscuits covered with a clean white cloth. Thanking them both for their kindness and about to take their gifts indoors and leave Eva and Elpida to go about their business, I realised I should ask them in for coffee. I ushered them inside and waved a circle to indicate they were free to walk round as they pleased. They nodded and started on what was really a tour of inspection. I put the biscuits on the table outside, the musmulas in the kitchen and filled up the kettle to make coffee. Oh dear, I had a briki but no ground coffee, only instant. Grabbing the coffee tin, I headed off to the bathroom where I could hear their voices. Expecting the worse and that they would be offended; I pointed to the tin with a very apologetic face. They just shrugged their shoulders as if to say it would be okay but I knew what would be on the top of my next shopping list. While they continued their inspection I laid a cloth on a tray before placing three cups and saucers, milk jug and sugar basin on top. The kettle boiled just as I finished and at the same time, Eva and Elpida made their way into the kitchen. I deduced from their nods and exchange of comments to each other that I had passed their inspection – phew! Cups filled, we made our way outside where my first real guests sat on the two veranda chairs while I brought a dining chair out to sit on. Elpida's biscuits were delicious with a tang of fresh lemons that complemented the bitterness of the coffee; even though it was only instant! Conversation was limited but I was able to answer their questions about where I came from and how long I was staying here and they were most tolerant of my pauses when I struggled to remember the right word and were extremely diplomatic when correcting my grammar and tenses. Before they left they walked round the garden where Eva indicated I would need to put in supports to tie the tomato plants to but apart from this everything seemed to be up their standards. I was relieved to have their approval. Why I don't know because ultimately I was only here for five months so what they thought was neither 'here nor there'. At the gate Eva invited me for coffee at her house the following week. This quite surprised me; I had been thinking they had only come for a 'nose' about. Shows how wrong you can be.

I said that Eva and Elpida were 'my first real guests' but that was not entirely true, that's if you count Rosie. I suppose it was bound to happen that before too long I would have an uninvited visitor of the feline kind. Once I had finished the cleaning and sorting the garden and settled into a slower pace of daily activities a small tortoiseshell female cat boldly walked up onto the veranda where I was sitting eating my breakfast. She did not introduce herself but strolled past me, straight into the house. My first thoughts were; fleas. All my labours and now the house would be infested with wretched fleas! I was hot on her heels ready to get the broom and 'sweep' her out of the door but I didn't. Why? Because I am drawn to cats, there is just something about them. Maybe it is because they are free agents and won't be accountable to anyone, which attracts me to them. I know some hate them because they are hunters and kill the birds and I cannot deny their method of tormenting their prey, before going in for the kill, is very cruel. Even so I have a sort of admiration for them and instead of sweeping her out the door; I relented and instead welcomed the small tortoiseshell. Whether she had been watching me from the surrounding fields and olive groves, biding her time and waiting for the right opportunity, I will never know but she had definitely decided to make Maria's house her home and me her servant! It's true what they say - 'Dogs have owners but cats have servants.' I named her Rosie because the lyrics of the first two verses of Don Partridge's song 'Rosie oh Rosie' were so her.

"Rosie oh, Rosie
I'd like to paint your face up in the sky
Sometimes when I'm busy
Relaxing I look up and catch your eye.

Your eyes when they're widening
Bring Thunder and Lightening
And Sunset strokes the colour of your skin"

That is except it should be 'colour of your fur' and not 'colour of your skin'. The next time I was in town I bought a stock of proprietary flea drops which she allowed me to administer without too much of a fuss and she settled into a fairly regular routine. She would spend her days in and around Maria's house, sometimes indoors curled up in the cool on a cushion on the long wooden settle or outside on one of the veranda chairs or in a shady spot in the garden. In the evenings she disappeared out hunting and would be waiting outside the door when I got up, ready to come in for her breakfast. I tried not to think what she would do when I went home at the beginning of October and I tried hard not to get attached to her but failed miserably on that score.

Stavros, Despina, Yiannis and Anna were gradually passing word around that I was here for the summer months but not everyone had heard. I began to get questioning looks when after two weeks I was still in the village and had not been picked up by one of the airport transfer coaches or taken a taxi to the airport, ready to start my journey home. By the end of my third week, I was getting quite skilled in replying 'Είμαι εδώ για πέντε μήνες, μέχρι τις αρχές Οκτωβρίου', 'I am here for five months, until the beginning of October'. There was one person who I did not have to reply to in Greek and that was the guy at the Hermes Car Hire office, who called out to me one evening, when I was walking back to Maria's house carrying two bags of shopping.

"Fancy a coffee?" he called across in a very definite Australian accent "I finish in half an hour; I'll meet you in the bar." he added, looking over at the aptly named 'Sunset Bar'.

Initial thoughts were, a bit presumptuous but then; why not? It would make a refreshing change talking to another English speaking person; that is other than general day to day chitchat with the tourists. Yes, it was all good practice speaking Greek and I was learning more pretty well every day but I found it could be a bit draining at times; listening intently then trying to compose a sensible answer. "Okay, see you in half an hour then." I replied and continued walking.

Back at Maria's house I put away the shopping. Considering there was just me and Rosie to feed it was surprising how much I bought on each trip to the supermarket. Well, I was still building up a bit of a store cupboard and the walk back from the tourist supermarket was downhill so not too arduous. I was thankful to Stavros who saved my arms by picking up and dropping off the bottled water on his way to his allotment. I looked at myself in the mirror, pulled a comb through my hair and decided that would do. Enough time to fill the moats round the tomatoes and peppers with water and I was off back up the track and road.

As the supermarket and tavernas etc. came into sight, I could see the guy from the car hire office; he was already standing outside the Sunset Bar. As I approached he held out his hand and with a powerful grip he shook mine at the same time introducing himself,

"Sorry, but you went off so quickly, I'm Bill and you are?"

"I'm Polly." I replied "Sorry but the bags were heavy and I was keen to get back and put them down."

We sat outside at a roadside table in the late afternoon sun and ordered frappés. Bill started the conversation,

"I have seen you passing back and forth for about three weeks now; obviously not a tourist, so I thought it would be good to have a chat and we could find out a bit more about each other. So let's start with you Polly, how long are you here for and what are you doing; repping or something?"

I told him the basics, like how I came to rent Maria's house through knowing Yiannis and his family from previous visits to the island and then pretty well the same as I told Anna; I had taken leave from work during a slack period. Bill was totally impressed that I had employers who had let me take five months off, even when they weren't busy. I then had to explain that I was the boss and really it was my employees who had agreed to hold the fort. I just hope that I sounded convincing to what was only a part truth. I had not told anyone yet the real reason why I was here and I was certainly not about to explain to someone who was basically a stranger.

Bill told me he lived between Brisbane and Sydney, on the outskirts of South West Rocks and worked in motor sales. There were a number of Greeks living in the area and that was how he got to hear about a summer job vacancy here; from a Greek friend who originated from Aspros. He told me he fancied a break and there were plenty of vacancies in motor sales in Australia so he wouldn't have any problem getting another job when he went home at the end of the season. He looked me up and down,

"Do you always wear shorts, t-shirt and walking boots?" he asked.

He sounded critical, what was it to him what I wore? What matters is I am comfortable, happy and relaxed in this attire. He got a short "Yep" as my reply, I certainly was not going to give him a run-down of my wardrobe and what I wore and when. I guess he realised he had pitched the question badly and came back with,

"Only, I like walking, so maybe we could take a hike out together some time. I don't get much time off, just the odd half day. What do you think?"

I wasn't sure what I thought about going off with some guy I had only just met but we agreed to take an early morning walk on the following Tuesday, not too far as he had to be back showered and ready to open the office at ten. Frappés finished and before we went our separate ways I knew I had to make things clear to him.

"Look Bill", I started, "I have really enjoyed talking and I want to go on this walk but you need to know, I am not looking for a relationship. If you are happy to be friends, go for walks, meet for a drink or have a meal in a taverna then that's fine but if you are looking for more then look elsewhere 'cos I'm not the girl for you." I paused and looked him in the eyes saying firmly, "You understand what I am saying?"

He was a bit taken aback, "Oh crikey yes, no that's okay, but somehow I didn't figure you were a lesbian."

I didn't know quite how to respond to that, I had without thinking, sent out completely the wrong message. After a brief pause, I broke into laughter. I mean, me a lesbian, if Amy had been here she would have had an attack of the giggles. I sorted the misunderstanding, I told him what I had been trying to convey which was; I was not here looking for a short term romance, I was not an easy lay and certainly not a Shirley Valentine character.

The walk went well; we took the path over to the ruined monastery of Aghios Dimitrios, a regular jaunt of mine and one which I always enjoyed. Some of the wild flowers were starting to die back, the grasses were setting seed and there were plenty of insects and butterflies to observe. We clambered over the monastery ruins, trying to imagine how it would have been before the earthquake had reduced it to a few erect walls, an arched doorway and piles of rubble. We seemed to have similar interests and Bill suggested we should make this a weekly event and take breakfast with us. We agreed that Thursdays would be a better day as this was changeover day and it would not matter too much if Bill was a few minutes late opening up the office in the morning.

Chapter 8

Before I left my business in the UK, in what I had hoped were the capable hands of my staff, we agreed that barring any emergencies they would not contact me for four weeks. There were times during those first four weeks when I was tempted to phone. It was Fiona that gave me cause for concern but I resisted and waited for the appointed day – Thursday 30th May. Back from my walk with Bill and after I had done a few chores, I settled myself in the privacy of the living room. It was coming up for midday; I was sat at the dining table, poised with paper and a pen, ready to take notes. At the same time I was keeping my fingers crossed that the phone signal would remain strong enough to receive the call. It was just after twelve when my mobile phone rang; it was Diane, the office accountant. She sounded quite excited and after asking me how things were going on Aspros, she announced that the contract, we had almost given up hope of securing with a Japanese company, had been signed. This was excellent news; such a valuable contract would increase our turnover by about 30%. I gave her my go ahead to hire another clerk and driver and to lease another van and; knowing my staff worked as a team and they all would have pulled together to impress the Japanese with their expertise, I felt this warranted a bonus for everyone. I suggested a ballpark figure to Diane and put her in charge of deciding the split before paying it through the payroll. This then brought up the subject of Fiona. She was in effect my joint partner and therefore Diane knew that before making the payments; she would have to run them past her for approval. Always to the point, Diane took over the conversation,

"Ah Fiona, well it won't come as any surprise to you that after you left, she continued to be her usual absolute pain in the rear end! She decided to go through the books once again; not that she understands the first thing about accounting. With you not around, this time she

45

centred on every single payment the company has made to you since you and Donald set the company up. She wanted to see all the back-up paperwork which meant going through all the files, some of which, as you know, are in storage. So help me Polly, I could have smacked her. I know she had been giving you a hard time but there we were splitting your work amongst us, keeping the business running smoothly, working on the Japanese contract and all this bloody woman, I know I shouldn't refer to her like that after what she's been through, but all she was interested in was questioning your expenses and director's payments. Anyway, this went on for about four or five days and since then we've hardly seen her, which of course is a total blessing. That was until this Monday when she breezed into my office and announced that the freight forwarding business was not for her, she wanted out and that just as soon as Donald's will had been through probate and his half of the company was legally hers, she was going to sell. So what do you think to that Polly?" Diane concluded.

I was horrified, who would she sell to? Would her half of the business get taken over by one of the 'big boys' and all the hard work Donald and I had put in setting up the company and marketing our services for its expertise and personal touch would just get sucked up and absorbed into their ways and methods? And what about the staff that had been so loyal and given that bit extra to help build us into the company we are now? And then I was cross. Cross with Diane for not phoning me straight away.

Before I could express my annoyance to Diane for her not phoning; after all this was an emergency, she resumed.
"I am sorry; I mean I am really sorry for not phoning you on Monday. Only you see when Fiona left, Tony came into my office to find out what she wanted. *(Tony was our top employee; he had been in the freight*

46

forwarding business for about fifteen years and would have taken over my top clients while I was away). I explained and basically neither of us wants things here to change, we are a good team, we work well together and now we have the Japanese contract we think we can grow the business further. A couple of coffees later we came up with - why don't **we** buy Fiona out. But before we could put this to you we both needed to examine our personal finances, talk to a solicitor and the bank. Well we've done this and we're up for it; so do you want to think it over? Do you want Tony and me as co-directors?"

I didn't need to time to think it over. This would be the perfect outcome; that was just so long as Fiona was in agreement to sell her half to Diane and Tony. I relayed my thoughts to Diane, she sounded relieved that I agreed and I left it with her and Tony to arrange a meeting with Fiona to put the proposition to her. The rest of the conversation brought me up to date on the business and just as we were about to hang up, Diane asked if there was anything I really missed about the UK. I had to laugh and told Diane,

"You just can't get a decent cuppa over here. It's coffee all the time and I really do like a mug of tea with my breakfast. I am going to ask Amy to bring a box of tea bags with her when she comes next week!"

We arranged that barring emergencies, Diane would phone again in a month's time and she would text me the outcome of the meeting with Fiona.

I went and sat out on the veranda with a glass of orange juice and went back over the contents of my conversation with Diane. So I was right, Fiona had built up in her mind, that it was my fault that Donald had committed suicide. Ever since his death she had been probing to find out more about our relationship. Whether we had been having an affair? Was the business in financial trouble? Was I taking more out of the business than Donald? It had become a grief driven obsession and it was having its toll on everyone. But now that I was out of the way and she had completed her delving, I presume she was satisfied I was not behind his death and she had now decided to sell, what would be her half of the business.

I knew that I shouldn't but I then went on to recall how I had come so close to what my doctor termed as a 'nervous breakdown'. After four weeks away from my daily routine and in a totally different environment, I felt the time was right and I could cope. Donald's death had a shattering effect on my state of mind. I was still low after my hysterectomy. I had thought myself a career girl and that changing nappies and sleepless nights were for the likes of Amy and not for me. I suppose the option was always there but choice was taken away from me when I was just thirty three. I started to dwell on what could have been; I started watching mums with their little ones in the supermarkets and in the park. Something I would never have dreamt of doing prior to the operation. I began to think about what I was missing, not the nappy changing of course, but all the pleasures of being a mum. It hit me hard and no doubt the change in hormone levels didn't help either. The only thing that seemed to work was keeping my mind occupied so I enveloped myself more and more in the business. When we were overloaded with work I waited until 6 o'clock and told everyone to go home, that included Donald. My reasoning was; they had families or commitments and I had none, well apart from Harry but he never seemed to mind what hours I kept. Sometimes I would stay until nearly midnight and would be back again just after seven the following morning. "What time did you leave?" Donald would ask. Pointless lying, I replied "Oh, 11.30'ish." My excuse for staying so late was invariably one of getting so absorbed in what I was doing that before I knew it the evening had gone. It is possible that staying so late had fuelled a suspicion in Fiona's mind that I was up to no good during those long evenings in the office.

If only Donald had left a suicide note, then there never would have been any of the ensuing speculations and suspicion. There was no question that he had committed suicide, nobody would take a whole bottle of prescribed sleeping tablets if their intention had not been to end it all. After the initial realisation had sunk in; that he was dead and would never come back into the office again, I went through a whole range of emotions. There was anger; why did he leave me with the business to run on my own. How selfish was that. There was guilt; was it something I had done which pushed him over the edge. And there was jealousy; Fiona, who I had never really gelled with and tolerated for the sake of the business relationship with Donald, was getting all the sympathy. A woman in her early thirties, widowed and left with two young children was bound to attract sympathy and it was totally wrong of me to expect compassion at the same level. But I did feel I deserved more consideration than I received, after all Donald and I had known each other since college days and had worked together for four years before setting up the freight forwarding company five years ago. Fiona's appearance in the office, delving into everything, did not help matters. I should have been more kind hearted but feeling as I did, I looked upon her visits as unnecessary intrusions. One thing for sure was; I could never forgive Donald for not leaving a suicide note; it was cowardly of him to leave this world without some kind of explanation.

They say things come in threes and the final blow came from Harry. Before I met Harry I had a number of boyfriends, none of which came up to my exacting standards. Some lasted a couple of months others I felt strongly enough about to rent a place and live with. Things then tended to fall apart and arguments followed. Too much sport, untidiness or general slovenly behaviour and the habitual toilet seat issues, were usually behind these disagreements. Then along came Harry, an artistic designer in the advertising business. He was kind, *thoughtful, generous, tidy, didn't follow sport, was the perfect gentleman and if that wasn't enough – he was drop dead gorgeous too. After living together for six months I knew he was the man I could spend my life with and when he proposed beneath the Copper Horse at the end of the Long Walk in Windsor Great Park, there was no doubt in my mind that I loved him and of course my answer was 'Yes'. We bought a flat, married, honeymooned on Aspros and carried on our lives as before. Harry's job took him away quite a lot and with me working long hours we tried to keep weekends as our time. This worked up to a point but invariably we were both tired come the end of the week and as time progressed; made love less frequently. That was until my operation when I completely lost my libido and love making ceased altogether. I thought Harry was being considerate and was waiting patiently but what I did not know was that he was seeing someone else – Mike. Harry 'came out' in February 2002, just six months after Donald had committed suicide and fourteen months after my hysterectomy. What I felt when Harry told me about Mike, I cannot put into words. To say my emotions were mixed is an understatement and after about a week without sleep, being totally irrational at work and with my mind in a total turmoil, Amy suggested I made an appointment to see my doctor. After the consultation and at Amy's insistence that I take my GP's advice, it took me just a matter of weeks to prepare for my five months here on Aspros.*

The strange thing is; I still love Harry. In a different way to the day we were married but he is such a gentle, caring and supportive man who has been through hell coming to terms with his sexuality and its effect on me, that I don't think I will ever be able to completely shut him out of my life.

After the morning's walk with Bill, the phone call from Diane and recollecting the past few years' traumas, I felt quite drained and after lunch opted for an afternoon on my own on the beach. After exchanging underwear for my swimming costume and with my beach towel (one of my purchases from the village supermarket) rolled round a bottle of sun lotion, I took a leisurely saunter down the twisting road to the beach. I had two delicious hours spent swimming, sunbathing and watching this week's new arrivals as they bailed out of taxis that had brought them down the last section of the road which was too narrow for the transfer coach. Their faces were a picture as they unloaded their cases from the boot of their taxi and stood looking at the stunning bay with blue seas and just a few apartments, villas and tavernas round its perimeter. You could almost hear their thoughts 'Amazing, it's just as the travel brochure described. It's perfect.' It was about four and I was thinking about walking back when Anna arrived with Kostas, Spiros and Karis. She had parked outside the family taverna and was making her way along the beach with the three children, all in their swimming gear. She smiled and waved when she saw me and came and sat down next to me. After the children had said hello, the two boys took hold of Karis's hands and walked across the sands and into the sea. They were so good with their two year old sister. I could understand six year old Spiros wanting to paddle and splash with her but I thought Kostas would have preferred to have been with his two older siblings. They were a joy to watch and I struggled to stop a pang of 'wanting' get to me. To divert my thoughts I chatted away to Anna. She told me that when Yiannis opened the Blue Sea at the beginning of June, any routine their lives had, would go out the window. Yiannis would be sourcing produce in the main town first thing in the mornings and would then be at the taverna for the rest of the day. He would not get home until nearly midnight and probably even later in August. All the day to day running of the house, looking after the family and garden as well as the studios would fall down to Anna. Once school was finished in mid-June, their two elder sons, Dimitri and

Christos would be working in the taverna or out and about with their friends, so they would not be around or want to be around, to give a hand with domestic chores. Not having to do the school run took a bit of pressure off Anna as well as the family eating their main evening meal in the taverna. It was having the two younger children pretty well tied to her apron strings that made life hectic.

"Last year", Anna explained, "I could fit in cleaning the studios on changeover day with Karis's morning nap but now she only sleeps for a couple of hours in the afternoon and when she is awake, I need eyes in the back of my head. It is going to be difficult. You don't want a cleaning or baby-sitting job do you Polly? No of course you don't, I was only joking."

I felt a little guilty not volunteering but I also had a thought which, for now, I kept to myself. Karis got bored with the sea and left the two boys splashing and swimming, in exchange for a cuddle wrapped in a towel.

I told her about Eva and Elpida turning up with musmulas and biscuits and how I could only offer them instant coffee and that Eva had invited me to her house next Tuesday. I asked whether I should take anything, some sort of gift.

"Of course" replied Anna, "I suggest home baked biscuits but a different type to those Elpida brought along. You can borrow one of my recipe books, if you like. Don't worry, I have a number of Greek/American books I brought with me from the States, so you won't have to sit and translate them!"

It was agreed that I would go back with them in the car, Anna would sort out a suitable book and I could then walk home from their house. After about an hour the boys too grew tired of the sea and they came back and sat with us on the sand. Anna gave them all a drink and biscuits to keep them going until dinner. I helped her fold up the towels and gathered up my towel and sun lotion before we all walked across the sands back to the car. Inside the Blue Sea, Yiannis was busy cleaning the kitchen area, he had already swept up the debris that had accumulated outside on the patio area and moved some of the tables and chairs outside. He waved and blew kisses from the window as we all clambered into the car. On the drive up the hill I told Anna I wanted my hair trimmed before Amy arrived the following Thursday and asked her if she knew of a good hairdresser. As luck would have it Anna was going into town to her hairdressers and to look at a wedding outfit on the Wednesday and offered to phone and see if she could get an appointment for me at more or less the same time. She said she would appreciate a second opinion about the outfit she had seen last week. I don't know if it was presumptuous of me but I suggested that maybe we could take Despina with us. She was progressing gradually and I thought a trip to the hairdresser would give her a boost. Anna thought this was an excellent idea and if she could get us both fitted in, she would drop by the following morning and let me know the times. I would then approach Despina and find out if it was convenient with her and Stavros; that was assuming she wanted to come at all. While Anna went indoors to find a recipe book, Kostas went off to the village square in search of a friend he had spotted and I played hide and seek outside with Spiros and Karis. Karis, not fully understanding how the game should be played, insisted that she was the one to hide each time and it was down to Spiros and I to do all the seeking. Karis kept giggling and giving her hiding place away, so Spiros and I had to pretend we could not find her, walking round the garden saying, "Όπου μπορεί να είναι;" "Where can she be?" After about half an hour when Spiros was obviously getting bored with the game, Anna emerged from the house with two books and a piece of paper.

"Hairdressers all arranged" she said, "I have jotted it down. I will pick you up at 10.30 a.m. on Wednesday morning; we'll stop for Despina and be in good time for yours and my appointments at 11.00 a.m. Maria is cutting your hair and will then style Despina's. You and I can go and have a look at the wedding outfit I was saying about and then go back for Despina. We should be ready for lunch by then; there is a good taverna on the waterfront. On the way back we'll stop and pick the kids up from school. It will be a bit of a squeeze but I am sure we can manage. Oh and Karis will come with us too."

It was left with me to run this past Despina and Stavros the following morning. I thanked Anna for the books, kissed Spiros and Karis goodbye and headed back to Maria's house where sat on the veranda was Rosie; waiting for her tea.

Chapter 9

The following morning, I walked purposefully up to Stavros's and Despina's shop; waving to shop and taverna owners and their staff as I passed. I stuck my head in the door of the car hire office to say good morning to Bill. He was just putting on the coffee machine to provide prospective customers with some refreshment while he checked availability of vehicles for their required rental period. As I continued, I thought how much I had enjoyed my first four weeks here and how I liked the feel of living in this village. Not a compact village by any means, with most of the tourist facilities about one kilometre down from the main road, the original village with its kafenion about half way down and finally the beach, lined with tavernas and more low key accommodations. I arrived at the shop just as they were opening. I was able to give a hand hanging the bags, hats, sarongs etc. outside. While we were doing so and in my best Greek (I knew basically what I wanted to say and had looked up beforehand the words I did not know in my dictionary), I told Despina about my conversation with Anna the previous afternoon but before I broached the subject of the hairdresser, I mentioned about how Anna was concerned as to whether she could cope with Karis on the studios changeover day. I was planting a 'seed' in Despina's mind, something for her to think about. Inside the shop I asked Despina if she would like to come with us to the hairdressers the following Wednesday. I hoped Stavros would not think I was interfering; he looked a little disgruntled at first but then when he saw Despina's face light up as she gasped, "Ω ναι παρακαλώ", "Oh yes please", he mellowed and assured her he could hold the fort for a few hours. Despina insisted I stop for a coffee (boy, I couldn't wait for Amy's arrival - complete with tea bags that is!) before I returned to Maria's house to write down next week's itinerary and ideas of what Amy and I could do when she arrived on the 6th.

After recapping on how I had come to be on the verge of a breakdown, I realised just how much I owed Amy for the support she had given me, throughout what had been and still was a difficult period for me. With a growing family, home and husband she still found time for me. She must have inwardly groaned at times when I phoned her – again. I was determined to make her visit a big thank you and above all a holiday where she could do what she wanted, when she wanted to. In the absence of any family, she had been in effect a sister to me; it was the least I could do.

Over the next couple of days, using recipes from Anna's books, I baked some Greek style shortbread and coconut biscuits from one book and almond biscuits from the other. I scaled down the ingredients but even so each batch made between 20-25 biscuits. That was a lot of biscuits for one person! I took a few up for Bill to try; he was so impressed with the almond ones I promptly walked home and brought back half of the batch and told him to give them to customers with their coffee. I asked the tourists who stopped at the gate for a chat if they would like to try some Greek biscuits; handing them some wrapped in a serviette. This was on the understanding that they would give me feedback on which they preferred or whether they were so awful they had fed them to the goats! It was not long before I had just a few left for myself but I could not decide whether the shortbread had the edge over the almond biscuits or vice versa. Most of the tourists agreed with Bill, so I baked almond biscuits to take to Eva's on Tuesday.

I wasn't quite sure what to expect as I walked along the track to Eva's house with my plate of almond biscuits, covered with one of Maria's hand embroidered cloths. As I approached Eva's garden gate I could hear voices from inside, not just one or two but a number. I nervously knocked on the part open door and all went quiet inside. Eva soon appeared and beckoned me into the living room where to my astonishment sat six ladies on various styles of chairs, which were arranged around the perimeter of the room. I handed Eva the plate of biscuits which she put on the table to join several other plates, while I walked across and shook hands with each of the women. I wasn't sure if this was correct but it felt right that I should introduce myself to each one individually. I struggled to remember their names, it was difficult so I decided to relate names to something specific about them; Maria-Anna had white hair, Fotini had a large mole on her right cheek, Rhea wore glasses, Maria had the largest ear lobes I have ever seen, Haris had a rather pronounced double chin and finally there was Elpida who I had met last week. They were all sixty years plus and apart from Rhea were, to put it politely, of ample proportions. Introductions made I sat down while Eva handed round coffees (only a few days now until tea bags would be winging their way here with Amy!) and then the biscuits. I don't know whether this was some sort of a competition but the four different types of biscuits were nibbled and comments passed, none of which I understood apart from 'Καλά', 'Good' or 'Πολύ καλά', 'Very Good'. I was relieved when my almond biscuits received positive expressions, nods of approval and a 'Καλά'. I sat drinking my coffee and eating biscuits while they chatted away, they spoke so quickly I could not grasp what was being said but I smiled politely and tried to look interested in their conversations. After about an hour Fotini stood up walked over, shook my hand and said, 'Αντίο', 'Goodbye' before saying farewell to the other ladies and leaving. Shortly after Maria-Anna, Haris, Maria and Rhea departed too leaving just myself, Elpida and our hostess Eva. I helped them clear away, taking plates, cups and saucers into the kitchen but they refused when I offered to help with the washing up. I picked up my empty plate and the cloth and said goodbye, leaving them to it. Well that was strange, I thought to myself as I walked back to Maria's house, what was that all about. In a way, I hoped I didn't get invited again; I needed a far greater grasp of the

language if I was going to enjoy their coffee mornings to
the full.

Chapter 10

The following morning Anna picked me up as arranged. Despina was waiting outside the shop and waved when she saw the car approaching. She was delighted to see us and insisted on sitting in the back where Karis was strapped into her child seat. Despina spent most of the drive into town talking to Karis who I could hear chuckling away. I had brought Anna's recipe books with me and told her about the coffee morning the previous day. She laughed and told me I had done well. Word had filtered back to her about the well-mannered English woman who shook hands with them and how it was considered Eva should not have any problems having me for a neighbour during the summer months. Anna explained that coffee mornings like these were usually reserved for the winter months, when there was more time for socialising and when doors were open to anyone who cared to pop in for a chat. This had been a one off special so that they could all have a good look at the English woman living in Maria's house.

Once in town, Anna parked the car in a side road off the square. Karis was none too pleased when she saw she was to be confined to her pushchair but after some coaxing from Despina she allowed herself to be strapped in. While Anna and I had our hair washed, trimmed and blow dried, Despina took Karis off for a walk round the shops. When they returned Karis proudly showed Anna a book which Despina had bought her.

"I thought it would keep her amused while you go and look at that wedding outfit." Despina offered as an explanation for the purchase but I could see that Despina was truly taken with Karis and had just wanted to buy her a present.

We left Despina explaining how she would like her hair to look and took Karis with her book off to the dress shop. The outfit was for a family friend's eldest daughter's wedding that was to take place in October; after all the tourists had gone home. Anna who usually wore jeans and t-shirts was totally transformed when she walked out of the changing room wearing the dress and jacket that had taken her eye the previous week. She walked on her toes, which pulled up her leg muscles and gave the effect of wearing heels. The dress was bright pink, short sleeved and peplum in style with the neckline, hem and sleeves bordered in purple. The jacket too was bright pink, edged in purple and fitted perfectly just above the dress's short overskirt.

"What do you think?" she asked, "Be honest please. Am I too old to wear the skirt above my knee? Does it look tarty from the back? I mean is it too tight over my bottom?"

Well it was just a little loud but I knew how the Greeks love to dress up on special occasions, so I kept this thought to myself.

"No" I replied "It fits just perfectly and you look great. Absolutely stunning in fact."

Anna smiled in appreciation of my comments. The shop assistant brought out a pair of shoes, a hat, fascinator and handbag in coordinating colours. The shoes fitted, the handbag was a perfect size for such an occasion and after a little bit of indecision, Anna settled for the fascinator. As one final safeguard, Anna asked the assistant if she could return the outfit if Yiannis did not approve; no problem, providing she did so within three days. All that was left was for the assistant to package everything and for Anna to pay. Everything was beautifully wrapped in tissue paper and put into elaborate boxes and tied with ribbon. Anna balanced the box with the dress and jacket on top of Karis's pushchair and I carried the boxes containing the shoes, handbag and fascinator. We took everything back to the car before returning to the hairdressers. I was pleased with the way Maria had cut my hair but she had totally transformed Despina. Her hair, that had been dragged back off her face and tied at the back, was now styled and shaped round her face with a feathered fringe. Despina's face said it all, as she announced,

"Lunch is on me!" Anna and I fussed round her, admiring her new look; it was the boost Despina needed.

We lunched at the waterside taverna, recommended by Anna, sharing a bowl of Greek salad, a large plate of small fish (gavros) and a basket of bread. We ate the fish with our fingers and mopped up the last of the salad juices and olive oil in the bowl with bread. We made a fuss of Karis and took it in turns to feed her; cutting up the child sized chicken souvlaki Anna had ordered for her and popping the small pieces into her open mouth. Throughout the morning Anna had done a fair bit of translating but my Greek was improving and it was while Karis was sat on Despina's lap that I managed to steer the conversation towards changeover day and how it would be difficult for Anna with Karis in tow. I sat back and waited to see if Despina had given any more thought to the 'seed' I had sown in her mind. I could not fully understand their conversation; I had to rely a lot on their facial expressions and body language. First there was Anna's concerned look as she explained her predicament, then Despina gestured to herself and then Karis with a questioning look towards Anna whose face almost immediately lit up. Anna got up from the table, walked round and hugged Despina who in turn landed a whopping kiss on Karis's cheek. Anna, still beaming, told me that normally on Thursday change-over day, Despina would be cleaning their studios ready for the new arrivals but because of her operation, this year the job had fallen to Stavros. Despina had offered to look after Karis in the shop, which of course would be quiet on Thursdays. If I could, I would have given myself a pat on the back – seed sown and germinated, Anna's problem solved and I would not feel guilty for not offering to babysit or do the cleaning!

We were late arriving at the school, I imagined an irate stern faced teacher waiting in the playground but it seemed commonplace for parents to be delayed. The children just waited or played outside until they did arrive. When they saw the car pull up, Anna's four strolled across but as soon as Dimitri saw the vehicle was already half full; he threw up his arms, shouted something to Anna and walked away.

"He's coming back later with a friend." she laughed. "He doesn't fancy playing sardines!"

Books thrown into the boot area, Christos sat in the front while Kostas and Spiros squeezed in the back with Despina, Karis and me. It was not too bad as Karis sat on Despina's lap where she held her safely against her body. I thought how different this Greek school was to my school days when nobody stayed a second longer than they had to. Here the school's playground and field were open throughout the day and even in the holidays. It provided an area where friends from surrounding villages could congregate and socialise.

Back in Lionas, we stopped to drop Despina off at the shop and then further down the road I got out at the supermarket. It wasn't the supermarket I really wanted but I did just pop in for some kitchen roll before I stuck my head round the door of the car hire office where Bill was sat inside working on some papers. He looked up, smiled and said,

"Hair looks nice; all you need is a bit of slap (make-up) and you would look quite presentable."

I had only known him a short while but knew not to take these remarks seriously.

"Ha! Ha!" was my response, followed by, "With Amy arriving tomorrow, not going to fit in the walk in the morning. Fancy going for a short walk and then going 'Dutch' someplace this evening instead?"

"Sounds good." was his response, "I've got a car coming back at eight thirty, should get away by nine, so maybe just eat without the walk?"

We agreed I would meet him at the office at nine and take it from there.

Returning to Maria's house I made up the bed in the spare bedroom ready for Amy's arrival. It looked a bit austere so I took a couple of colourful hand painted china jugs out of a cupboard and put them on the chest of drawers. In the morning I would fill these with wild flowers and grasses from the field behind the house. I then spent time in the garden; making sure that everything was up to date so that all I would have to do over the following week was to water. There was plenty of time to hoe the vegetable plot, check the tomatoes for side shoots, dead head the roses and give everything a thorough watering. Next on the list was a shower; I put on jeans, a new lightweight pink jumper I had bought in town a couple of weeks back and finally a bit of slap before sitting on the veranda with my diary and usual glass of wine. Opposite me was Rosie curled up on the other chair. In the end I wrote very little in my diary as I was continually interrupted by tourists walking past. For most of them it was their last evening on Aspros and their last chance to satisfy their curiosity, if they had not already done so, as to why an English woman was living here. They could tell I was living on my own and was not a rep for a travel company and were intrigued. I didn't mind the intrusion but I did wonder if I should pin a notice on the gate to the effect 'I'm here on a sabbatical, until the beginning of October.' Walking past Georgios's on my way to meet Bill, I could see the taverna was quite quiet. Presumably those tourists who had flights first thing the following morning had eaten earlier on. My original thoughts were to walk down to the old village to eat but on second thoughts maybe we should eat here. The taverna in the old village was frequented by locals, who invariably ate later than the tourists but it was not worth taking the risk, in case they were closing by the time we arrived. Bill was locking up the office and he walked down to meet me. He had similar thoughts to mine and so we settled for a corner table at Georgios's. This way as the other tables emptied they could clear away without thinking they were disturbing our evening. I felt at ease in Bill's company and told him a bit about Amy, how we came to be friends and what I thought we could do over the coming week. I suggested that maybe we could spend an evening or two together and as Amy's return flight was not until the early afternoon, we decided, provided Amy was in agreement, that the three of us would take our usual Thursday morning walk to the ruined monastery complete with a picnic breakfast. This I hoped would make the most of Amy's last few hours on the island before the taxi took us to the airport.

Chapter 11

Thursday morning, I was up early as usual. After feeding Rosie and watering the garden and pots on the veranda, I shinned over the back wall and cut some of the fast fading wild flowers and grasses to put in Amy's room. Next on my list of things to do was to have a quick dust, mop the kitchen floor and finally walk down to the village shop where I knew I could buy delicious spanakopitas (spinach and cheese pies) for lunch; one of Amy's favourites. A couple of weeks ago I had arranged for taxi driver Thanassis to pick me up just before midday so that I would be at the airport around 12.15 p.m. Amy's flight was due to land at about 12.20 p.m., so in theory, taking into account disembarking and baggage reclaim Amy should walk through the arrivals door twenty minutes later. Thanassis promised to wait, which I thought was pretty good of him but asked me to let him know if there was a flight delay, in which case he might be able to squeeze in a fare to town. Thanassis pulled up outside Maria's house on time and although he drove fast; I was not too alarmed. He always managed to maintain one hand on the wheel, taking frequent sips from his frappe, which he took out of the cup holder on the dashboard, while in his other hand he held a cigarette which he drew from, flicking the ash out of the open window. Thanassis was obviously well aware of the varying road surfaces and the angle of the bends. As soon as we arrived at the airport I checked out the flight arrivals; Amy's flight was due to land five minutes early and as I went out to tell Thanassis I heard the airliner bringing Amy and a fresh intake of tourists, landing on the runway with a thud. Back in arrivals, I took my place, along with the holiday reps and taxi drivers, and waited in anticipation for Amy to emerge from customs and through the automatic sliding doors. After about fifteen minutes the doors opened and the first of the tourists walked through with their eyes scanning for their holiday company's rep. It was a pretty slick operation with names ticked off the rep's lists and tourists directed outside to the coaches that would take them to their accommodation. A few minutes later, out came Amy with a large handbag slung over her shoulder and dragging a small trolley case behind her. She looked a little flushed, her eyes were searching for me and then she beamed as she saw me walking towards her. I gave her a welcome hug before she stood back and looked at me.

"Wow, Polly" she said, "You look so well and so relaxed. If this is what Aspros has done for you; I think I should stay too!"

Aware Thanassis was waiting, I ushered her quickly into his waiting taxi.

On the journey to Lionas, we chatted away nineteen to the dozen. She told me the reason why she was so flushed was because a woman had insisted Amy's case was hers and it wasn't until a nigh on identical case came up on the carousel that the woman realised her mistake.

"I showed her my name tag on the case", explained Amy "but she just wouldn't have it and then when her case came up, with the holiday companies tag on it and we took it off the carousel she finally conceded. I was really annoyed and she never even apologised!"

By the time Thanassis pulled down the dirt track and stopped outside Maria's house, Amy had calmed down.

"Here we are," I announced "your home for the next seven days."

I paid and thanked Thanassis. He opened the boot and handed me Amy's case, turned the car round and disappeared up the track in a cloud of dust.

Amy stood by the gate.

"Wow" *(this was one of her favourite words)* she said, "It's just as I remember it when we walked past on one of our walks."

She spent the next ten minutes or so, walking round the garden and inside Maria's house. Every now and then I could hear her saying 'Wow'. I put her case in her room and opened all the shutters and windows so that the breeze could blow through and cool the house, then busied myself in the kitchen preparing a small salad to go with the spanakopitas. I had just finished when Amy came into the kitchen.

"This is just amazing, its beautiful." she exclaimed "I love it all and the garden is just to die for. Wow, when I get home, I am going to be thinking of you in this little house and out in the garden and I am going to be so envious."

We sat out on the veranda and relaxed over our lunch. After we had finished eating, Amy sat back in her chair and gazed through the tall Cyprus trees at the deep blue sea and as she did, I watched two salty tears roll down her cheeks.

"Oh my goodness." I said "Homesick and missing the family already?"

She wiped away the tears, "No, it's because I have been so worried about you. I kept wanting to phone but knew I mustn't. And now I am here and can see you looking so well and at home; it's been such a relief that I just got a bit emotional. But no more tears, what are we going to do this afternoon, can we go to the beach?"

I suggested she unpacked and changed while I cleared away and washed up and then yes a leisurely walk down to the beach would be the perfect start to Amy's week on Aspros. I had just finished clearing up when Amy walked into the kitchen smiling and holding a handful of post and two large boxes of tea bags.

"There you go." she said "Let me know when you start on the second box and I'll send some more to you."

"Lifesaver!" I replied "I've really missed my breakfast cuppa. I am just about coffee'd out. Thanks for the post but that will have to wait for now."

Alan had bought Amy a new camera for her birthday, which she was keen to try out. I don't know how many times we stopped on the way down to the beach so she could take photographs of flowers, lizards, bees, the village square, fresh vegetables displayed outside the shop and so on; she had an eye for framing and capturing. We spent the afternoon chatting on the beach, mainly about Despina, Anna, Bill, Rosie and what I had been doing in general. That was until we decided a drink was called for. Yiannis was just opening the Blue Sea, ready for the evening trade so we popped in to say 'Γεια σου', 'Hello'. He insisted we sat out on the patio, near the sea where as a welcome for Amy, he brought us glasses of chilled white wine and a plate of marinated olives. It was nearly seven before we left and started the walk up to Maria's house and half past by the time we arrived to be greeted by a very cross Rosie.

I had been in the habit of feeding her between five or six, so I was in big trouble. Instead of winding herself round my legs and purring, she was intent on scolding me for my tardiness. She meowed loudly and scowled and when I opened the front door, she marched straight into the kitchen, sat in front of the fridge and meowed again. A very angry Rosie tucked into the plate of food I put down for her. When she had finished, I asked her if she enjoyed her tea. She just looked up at me as if to say 'Yes it was nice – *when* I eventually got it.' and then turned tail, walked out and curled up on a chair on the veranda.

"Well' laughed Amy 'you have just been well and truly told off!"

Quick showers, followed by another glass of wine sat out on the veranda; by this time Rosie had gone off for an evening's hunting. While we sipped our wine, Amy phoned home and I opened my post, which contained nothing exciting, and scribbled a few notes in my diary. Amy wanted to see Georgios so this made the decision of where we would eat easy. He was delighted to see her, gave her a massive hug and told her he had been keeping an eye on me and then showed us to my favourite table; the one overlooking the roses. It was Amy's turn now to tell me her news, but first I gave her the jewellery I had bought for her birthday.

"You can change it, if you don't like it." I explained but as Amy opened the box I could tell she would not take up the offer.

"Wow", she exclaimed "They're absolutely gorgeous. I love them."

She immediately took off the jewellery she was wearing, put them in the box and put on her birthday present.

"There." she said "Wish I had a mirror though."

She brought me up to date on what her children Emily and Daniel had been up to and how the American company Alan was working for were so demanding and he was working all the hours imaginable. The children were hard work and without Alan coming home at the time most other husbands did she was taking the whole brunt of their tantrums, the 'I wants' and the 'I don't wants.' She told me, she had been so excited since her mum gave her the airfare to Aspros for her birthday. A break from the daily routine was just what she needed. Amy's mum had taken a week off work so she could look after the house and children in Amy's absence. Amy let out a deep sigh.

"With Emily now at school and Daniel at playgroup I was beginning to get things under control, then I missed a period and then had sore boobs and then nothing happened again last week, so that's two I've missed. No need to go to the doctors. I know I am up the spout again. So it's going to be back to nappies and sleepless nights! Alan was stunned but I think we are both coming round and accepting it now. It's just; it's not what we planned. I am certainly going to make the most of this break away from all my responsibilities."

Another sigh and Amy sat back in her chair.

Chapter 12

Amy wanted to 'make the most of this break' and that's what we did. I left her to sleep in most mornings while I fed Rosie, tended the garden, prepared breakfast, with mugs of tea of course and sometimes a picnic lunch too. It was getting warmer by the day but that did not deter us from strolling across to Aghios Nicholas beach to collect rock salt, a stiff hike across the hills that required an early start to the Monastery of Aghios Christoforos and a cross country walk to a small roadside taverna that served the most amazing chicken cooked in the oven. We took the bus to the main town for some retail therapy. Amongst other things, Amy bought Daniel a wooden train and we rounded the morning off with a coffee and baklava in the main square. A visit to Despina's and Stavros's shop was a must. Here Amy found a necklace made of small pink shells for Emily and a hand painted terracotta dish for her mum. Alan was more of a problem but she settled for a hat in the end, one he could wear when he was mowing the lawns; that was when he found the time. On a cooler cloudy day we decided to hire bikes, pushing them up to the main road before setting off in earnest. Up on the relatively flat tarmac we cycled through villages that clung to the hills, occasionally stopping to walk up through the cool twisting lanes where the smell of cooking emanated through open windows along with strains of music from radios. There was a surprise visit one early evening from the ever nosey Eva and of course, we found time for the beach where Amy, in her bikini, asked for assurance that her pregnancy 'didn't show'. We ate out every evening, a couple of times with Bill and were invited by Anna to join their family meal at the Blue Sea. As they tended to eat later, Amy and I had consumed a few glasses of wine beforehand and with the wine drunk over dinner, we were both mellow by the time we set off to walk back up the hill. But we did so, initially striding out to work off the alcohol, slowing later to take time to look up at the stars and stopping to watch the glow worms. I kept a watchful eye on Amy; being pregnant, I was not sure that she should have drunk so much. She must have observed my concern because she told me that her mother had drunk throughout her pregnancy with her; the advice at the time was drinking alcohol was fine so long as you didn't get totally legless. However, she did concede that once she had been to the doctors she would stop because if this pregnancy was anything like the other two; the change in hormones tended to make her emotional over absolutely nothing. I remembered this well, in particular after an evening out with Amy and one of her bumps. We had a bottle of wine with our dinner; for no apparent reason she was reduced to floods of tears on the journey home and was inconsolable for about an hour.

It didn't seem long before Bill was at the door complete with picnic breakfast ready to walk over to Aghios Dimitrios. It was Amy's last day. She was unusually quiet as we set off along the track. After a while she told me,

"I am so chilled, this has been a wonderful week, it's been such fun and a great tonic but I am actually beginning to miss the kids and even more so, Alan. I am looking forward to seeing them when I land this evening and of course I have masses of wonderful photographs to show and bore Alan with. Now I have seen how you have embraced your life here and have people like Bill, Georgios, Despina and Anna to keep an eye on you and help, if you need it, I no longer have to worry. Even so, it is going to be sad to leave this beautiful island."

She made me promise to use the internet café on the outskirts of town where we could exchange news via emails. This made sense as I could keep in touch with the office and check how Diane and Tony were progressing with the purchase of Fiona's half of the business. Breakfast was eaten, sat on the rim of what we deduced was an olive mill, where ripe olives from the surrounding groves would have been crushed by the monks and where the green oil would have flowed out through a gap and into containers. Bill had driven to the bakery first thing and knowing Amy's passion for spanakopita had bought four slices. One slice for each of us to eat for breakfast and the remaining slice for Amy to either take home or eat on the plane. Amy laughed, there was no way she was going to share when she got home and said, she would devour it on the plane while all the other passengers ate their inflight meals. She added, if she developed cravings for spanakopita she would tell Alan; Bill was to blame! Bill had also bought juicy red tomatoes, yoghurt, chopped fresh fruit and a container of orange juice that had been freshly squeezed at the village shop that morning. When it was laid out Amy said,

"Wow, do you breakfast like this every Thursday morning?"

"Pretty well" I replied "but the spanakopita is usually substituted with bread and cheese or cold meats. It keeps us going most of the day, doesn't it Bill?"

"Sure does." he confirmed "Far better than a bowl of cereal!" he laughed.

Amy had already packed so we had plenty of time for one last walk up through the village. Bill went off to shower and change and as he walked up the alley towards his studio, Amy stopped. She turned towards me saying,

"He seems a really nice guy Polly. I know you're not up for another relationship but if you wanted more than friendship; well, I think you two could make something out of it."

I was a little annoyed at her remark. That Amy should even suggest, in my current frame of mind, that I could want more than friendship, did not go down well. I knew she would want some kind of response so I settled for,

"We are fine as we are. There is no question that either of us wants anything more."

Sensing she had rattled me and wanting to change the subject, Amy suggested we walk up to the café a bit further along the road so she could enjoy a final frappé.

Thanassis picked us up from Maria's house just after midday and whizzed us to the airport. Amy's flight had just started to check-in and I stood with her in the queue. It was a very silent affair, everyone going home and back to their daily routines. There was little to say as they shuffled their cases towards the check-in desks. The luggage x-ray scanner was just before the check-in desks and at this point I left Amy and waited near the café. When Amy joined me we bought cokes and checked the departure board; her flight was due to leave on time. Strange really, we had spent the last week chatting away and now we had run out of conversation. It was not long before passengers on Amy's flight were told to go through passport control. There was no rush but Amy said it was best to say goodbye now. She knew Thanassis was waiting for me and she said it would give her plenty of time to look round the tax free shop. So we said our goodbye's, shed a few tears and Amy walked to passport control, turning and waving before she disappeared into the departure lounge.

I felt deflated; only to be expected I suppose. Outside there was no sign of Thanassis; I guessed he had picked up a fare from an incoming flight. I found a bench in a shady spot and waited. It was about twenty minutes before he drove into the car park to take me home. 'Home', this was the first time I had referred to Maria's house as home; now there was a thought. Thanassis apologised for keeping me waiting; I told him it was not a problem. We travelled back exchanging a few comments about the weather and Thanassis cursed a couple of times at hire cars, who according to him were driving too slow. He pulled up at the garden gate where I paid and gave him a generous tip. Rosie was curled up in the shade, getting up to greet me with a meow. There was a note pinned to the door saying 'Join us for dinner at the Blue Sea tonight. Love Anna.' She must have guessed I would be feeling a bit flat and thought dinner with the family would liven me up. I heard the distant rumbling of a jet engine and looked at my watch, yes that would be Amy; on her way home. I hoped I had achieved what I set out to do; to give her a week to remember that would go some way towards saying thank you for all she had done for me in the past.

Chapter 13

There was plenty to do to keep me occupied until the evening. I started by stripping Amy's bed and putting the linen in the washing machine. I then set to, giving the place a clean and catching up with my laundry. Late afternoon, when the temperatures were cooler, I hoed the vegetable plot, weeded the rose bed at the front and gave everything a good watering round the roots. I tried to avoid watering the foliage in case there was still enough strength in the sun to scorch the leaves. Back inside the dust from the garden had stuck to the sun lotion on my legs; I felt generally hot and sticky. Time for a shower but before I did; there was a message on my phone. It was from Amy. 'Good flight. Ate the spanakopita! In baggage reclaim. Thanks for a great week. Will email in a day or so. Take care. xx' Good, Amy was safely back in England and no doubt Alan and the kids would be there waiting with welcoming hugs. Seemed strange that just a few hours ago we were having breakfast with Bill, sat on the old olive mill.

That reminded me, I had not eaten since breakfast. No point in eating too much now, so after my shower I settled on the veranda with Rosie along with a glass of retsina and a packet of oregano crisps. For the past week I had just entered single words in my diary, leaving the padding out until Amy had gone home. I spent an hour or so filling in details and realising how much we had packed into the week. With this complete I set off for the beach, arriving much too early for dinner but with time for a barefoot walk along the sands and a paddle. As I turned the last bend before the beach I could hear music being played; it was coming from the Blue Sea. In one corner of the patio, I could see three musicians sat playing and singing. Yiannis had arranged for an evening of traditional music. An excellent strategy on his behalf; bringing in new arrivals and something different for those who were just starting the second week of their holiday.

The place was full, not a spare table to be seen. I could see Yiannis and Dimitri working hard in the kitchen and Anna, Christos and Kostas seemed to be struggling to keep pace with taking orders, serving and clearing tables. What should I do, go for that walk along the sands, or help? No choice really; I went into the kitchen grabbed an apron and started on the washing up. The stacks of plates and dishes and rows of glasses on the shelves were dwindling fast and with tables filling as soon as they became vacant it was obvious they would soon run out. The pile next to the sink was considerable to say the least but I set to and within twenty minutes I had made sure there was enough crockery to keep the flow of plates from kitchen to table. It was about another hour and a half before things started to quieten down and Anna came into the kitchen and hugged me saying,

"Can't thank you enough Polly, we were sinking fast!"

There was an extractor in the kitchen and ceiling fans too but the heat from the cookers and hot plates made it almost unbearable. Sweat was running down the back of my neck, my hair felt damp and my top was sticking to me but we were all the same; even Anna and the boys who were working outside suffered too. But where were Spiros and Karis? Anna took me into a small room to the side of the kitchen area where there was a bed with Spiros and Karis curled up fast asleep. The bed was used in the afternoons during high season by Yiannis; somewhere where he could grab an hour or so sleep before preparing for the evening trade. The evening was a total success and it was past eleven before everything was cleared away and everyone, including the musicians, sat down to eat. Basically we ate what was left over; surprisingly there was a great selection of dishes and plenty for us all. Yiannis insisted we just piled the dishes in the sink and leave them overnight to soak. Nobody argued; we were all pretty bushed by then. Spiros and Karis were carefully lifted from the bed onto the laps of the older children in the back of the car and I gratefully accepted Yiannis's offer to drive me home after taking the family back to their beds. Another shower was called for before I fell into bed and sank into a deep sleep.

Surprisingly I woke in the morning at the normal time. I wondered if Anna was managing to get the children up and ready for school after their late night at the taverna. If she was struggling, it would not be a problem for the coming weeks as today was Friday 14th June and the end of term. I presumed that over the coming weeks, providing they had a siesta in the afternoon, they would be able to cope with working in the taverna and the resulting late nights.

It was getting hotter by the day and I was beginning to think a siesta was something I might consider over the coming weeks. It was while I was contemplating the siesta idea when Anna stopped by with Karis. She was on her way back after taking the children to school and was apologetic about the previous evening. I told her I was pleased to help out and had really enjoyed sitting down with the musicians and family to eat and how good the food was. I asked her how Yiannis managed to make the potato salad taste so good.

"He adds a good slug of ouzo, for added flavour!" she smirked.

Starting the following week, they had a couple of Dimitri's friends coming to help with serving, washing up and clearing tables but Anna said if ever I was at a loose end they would always be pleased of another pair of hands in exchange for dinner at the end of the evening. In the end I agreed to come on a regular basis on Thursday evenings. So my Thursdays would start with a walk with Bill in the morning and a siesta in the afternoon in preparation for a long evening at the Blue Sea.

I don't know whether it was a good thing or not but I started to build a regular weekly routine. On Mondays I took the bus into town to pick up and answer emails which generally left me enough time for some shopping in the supermarket.   Tuesday mornings I devoted to housework and washing. Wednesday, when Stavros did general repairs to their studios and a couple of villas in the hills, I spent most of the day helping Despina. Thursday I walked with Bill first thing and then helped at the Blue Sea in the evenings. This left Friday, Saturdays and Sundays to do as I pleased which usually involved, walking, time on the beach and I had taken an interest in cooking.   I borrowed some books from Anna and experimented with some traditional dishes.   The only problem was the quantities. I did not want to be eating the same thing for about four days running, so I started taking up portions for Bill in exchange for honest feedback and occasionally I invited Eva to join me for dinner. I think she quite enjoyed the company and she gave me many helpful ideas. She didn't drink alcohol but made wonderful lemonade which she brought with her for us to drink. The thing I liked about Eva was that although she was rather nosey she never criticised my cooking or gardening efforts, instead she would make suggestions which in anybody's book, are so much better received.

On the Monday after Amy's return home, I took the bus into town to access my emails. There were two, one from Diane which was just 'testing'. Amy must have told her I could now be contacted this way and Diane was making sure I could pick up her messages before sending anything lengthy. The second was from Amy which went as follows. *'As you know, I arrived safely at Gatwick. No problems this end with baggage reclaim! Hugs and kisses from Alan and the kids in arrivals. Mum absolutely knackered poor thing; the kids had worn her out. Alan has been extremely attentive and we spent that first night home locked in each other's arms. I hadn't realised how much I missed him. While I was away, he told his American bosses that he needs more help. After spending a year getting the new UK subsidiary off the ground, he told them he needed an assistant and someone to run the office. They threw a wobbler so he gave his notice in, which did the trick because they have told him to go ahead and recruit and given him a salary increase too! Oh and one other thing, he is fed up with the UK agents they appointed so he has contacted Diane and Tony and asked them if they would like to quote for the business. Alan says he is determined to be more of a nine till five father as he is missing out seeing the kids grow up. Life is looking so much better Polly, even the kids are behaving better but not sure how long that will last for! I have made an appointment to see my GP later this week and I actually think I am going to enjoy pram pushing again. Finally, I can't apologise enough for the remark about Bill. It was totally thoughtless of me. Please forgive me. Look forward to hearing your news. Love Amy xx p.s. I have some wonderful photos taken on my new camera of Aspros. No point sharing, as you see it all every day!!'*

Towards the end of June I began to think about Harry's and Mike's arrival on the 11th July. Not only would it not be fair on them to stay with me but also I was not sure I was quite ready to be thinking of Harry in the next room with his protective arms locked round Mike. Instead I decided to ask Stavros and Anna if either of them had a vacant studio that week. There was also the question of explaining Mike, they both expected Harry to be coming on his own and so far I had done nothing to dispel this. I first asked Stavros if he had anything I could rent for a couple of my friends but all his studios were full. I then asked Anna who immediately offered me one of their studios, it was one of two on the top floor which they kept vacant in case friends or family wanted to visit and as I was a friend and nobody else had indicated they wanted to visit that week; my friends were welcome to use it. She explained that it was the best of the six studios. At the front and on the top floor, it had the best views across the bay and sea and it was also better equipped than the other five. For insurance purposes, she said she would need their names. She then went on to question; wasn't this the week that Harry was coming to stay and were they friends of ours? I had managed successfully to avoid the topic of Harry's visit; now it was time to explain.

As I told Anna various looks went across her face; horror, anger and then finally sympathy. What she found difficult to understand was that I actually still wanted to see Harry and even more so, that I could accept him being with Mike. I tried to explain to her how I still loved Harry and that basically he had not set out to hurt me; neither of them had but all the same it had been a great shock. In the end she just shrugged her shoulders and gave me a reassuring hug saying that she looked forward to welcoming them.

Oh dear, was their visit as a couple going to be accepted. Maybe I should never have agreed to their coming in the first place. I was thrown into a quandary. I did not want them ostracised from shops and tavernas. I knew gay couples, both male and female, had stayed in Lionas without there seeming to be any problems but this was slightly different. I suppose Anna's concerns stemmed from the fact that Harry and I had spent our honeymoon here. I wasn't too sure what was the best way forward. In the end, about a week before their arrival, I told Stavros, who translated and told Despina and I also told Bill, Georgios, Sophia and Aris. I didn't imagine it would be a problem for Bill but hoped it would give the others time to think and 'fingers crossed' they would accept them as they would any other gay couple.

Chapter 14

July saw the daytime temperatures rise well above 30°C and the early mornings and nights were no longer cool. I stopped shutting both windows and shutters when I went out; instead I pulled the curtains and fastened the shutters in the hope that any breeze would blow through into the rooms. I spent more and more time outside in shady areas of the garden and bought a barbeque to cook on. Grilled meats, with salads from the garden, were regulars on my weekly menu. If I went to the beach I generally went down late afternoon, after my siesta and did not return until early evening. Walking back up the hill, I stopped in the old village to buy a refreshing drink to sip whilst sat under spreading branches of the plane tree. Perspiration poured off me when I did the housework and tended the garden and my whole daily routine shifted. Sunrise was after 6 a.m. but there was always sufficient light just after five for me to be able to go out and water the garden. Apart from the occasional passing local on their way to their allotment garden, there was nobody about so I never bothered to get dressed and went out in my nightdress and flip flops to puddle water round the base of the plants and flood the trenches where the carrots and salad vegetables were growing. By eleven I stopped any physical work in favour of sitting reading a book on the veranda. If I set off on a walk after sunrise I tried to make sure I was back no later than midday. Early in the morning snakes slithered across the paths and lizards sat on dry stone walls, warming their bodies. The wild flowers had all died back, leaving the floors of the olive groves brown and gold. Such a contrast to May when they were full of greens, yellows, reds and blues. It was the same along the perimeters of the paths and tracks and as the seed heads formed I took advantage and picked some to take back with me for Amy to plant in her garden. I had already picked two good sized bunches of oregano which were now, under Eva's instructions, split into smaller bunches, tied and hung to dry from the trellis work above the veranda.

I ate lunch between midday and one and then settled down on my bed for a couple of hours sleep. It was more like dozing than sleeping as the cicada's constant raucous chirping often woke me. I never felt particularly refreshed after these siestas; sleeping during the day had never agreed with me but it proved to be a necessity. I had to accept that after I got up, it would take me about half an hour to get my act together. Sitting on the veranda with a mug of tea usually did the trick and just as soon as I thought of what I needed to do, such as shopping etc., I regained my normal thought process. I now rarely ate before nine in the evening; it was just too hot to cook any earlier. The lamp on the veranda shone enough light down onto the garden to cook on the barbeque and citronella candles dotted about, provided a relaxed atmosphere and kept the mosquitos at bay.

To save on water, I used the washing machine for bed linen and towels only and hand washed my clothes which weren't especially dirty, just dusty and sweaty! Although there were no problems with water supplies I felt better in my own mind that I was using the washing machine sparingly, pouring the water from my hand washing and rinsing round the roses. Everything dried in no time at all; even the hand washing which I wrung with my hands rather than spinning in the washing machine. I went to bed around midnight, often later on Thursdays when I had been helping at the Blue Sea and I slept either on top of the bed or with just a sheet over me. Stavros kindly made wooden frames with mosquito netting that fitted inside the window frames, so I had little problem with these pesky little insects getting in while I slept.

Had I been expected to hold down a job while handling the heat; I am not sure I could have coped. Bill was fortunate, there was air conditioning in the office and the only time he needed to venture outside was to check over the cars returned at the end of their rental period before vacuuming and washing them ready to go out on the road again. As this was usually late afternoon to early evening he said he was fine and could manage. Life took on a slower pace, not that it was ever really hectic here on Aspros. Even Eva, who normally bustled down the track on her daily trip to the shop, took to gently strolling, stopping every now and then to mop her brow with her handkerchief whilst mumbling to herself about the heat.

Chapter 15

I phoned Harry to tell him about the revised accommodation plan. He seemed a little disappointed at first but when I told him they would be staying in one of Anna's studios, he sounded quite pleased, especially as the studios were just behind the beach and they would be able to go for early morning swims. I made the same arrangements with Thanassis as I had for Amy. There was a slight flight delay of half an hour which Thanassis took advantage of and picked up a fare to the inland hamlet of Davgata. He was back by the time Harry, Mike and I walked out of arrivals. Anna had dropped the studio keys off earlier in the morning on her way with Karis to Despina's. This way Thanassis could drive us straight down towards the beach, taking the narrow dirt track that leads to the back of the studios. On our way Mike told me about the photography contract he had landed and how because of this he was very nearly not able to come with Harry. After having heard so much about Aspros from Harry he was terribly disappointed but thankfully he had been able to reschedule the shooting. Harry had been just as busy in the advertising world. As Thanassis turned the taxi towards the back of the studios, they both said that was enough and there was to be no more talk of work during their holiday.

I took them up the outside stairs to their studio. Behind me I could hear them puffing as they lugged their cases over each marble step. I opened the studio door so they could manoeuvre their cases straight inside. It was traditionally furnished with separate kitchen, bathroom, lounge and bedroom, the latter two each with their own balcony; it was more of an apartment than a studio. Anna had added a few personal touches that family and friends would appreciate. They were quite thrilled with the accommodation. I nudged Harry and whispered,
"Let Mike open the curtains and shutters."

"Bit gloomy in here." Harry said "You'd better open the shutters Mike and let a bit of light in."

Mike gasped as he folded the shutters back onto the balconies and the full vista of the bay came into view. He was lost for words for a few seconds; this was something for Mike as he was never quiet for any length of time. It was not long before he was spouting out a string of adjectives – beautiful, spectacular, awesome, stunning etc. Harry looked at me and smiled before walking to put his arm round Mike's shoulders,

"Told you it was something else, didn't I?" Mike looked up into Harry's eyes,

"You did but I never imagined it would be quite like this. It's a photographer's dream." he sighed.

I kissed them both goodbye, told them I would be helping at the Blue Sea that evening where there would be live music but they were to come up and eat at my place on Friday evening. I told them we would have a barbeque and they could sample some of the produce from my garden. Just before I left, Harry unzipped his case and produced a small bundle of mail that had accumulated in the flat since Amy's visit.

I took a steady walk up the hill, stopping to buy a bottle of water in the village. I took a few good gulps before continuing. Any kind of exertion in this heat made me thirsty. As I walked I flicked through the envelopes. Mostly, the senders were fairly obvious and I was glad Harry had not wasted his baggage allowance by bringing junk mail. There was one envelope which I pondered over. It was small, the size that matched writing paper and handwritten. Although I was intrigued as to whom it was from, I decided not to open it until I got home. Rosie was curled up in the shade on one of the chairs on the veranda, I put the envelopes on the table and went inside and poured myself a glass of squash before joining her. I left the handwritten envelope until last and opened it with care. For years I had wondered if a letter like this would come through the door, but once I was in my mid-twenties I had discounted the possibility. I always knew what my response would be - *if* a letter ever came. There were two pages, written in well-formed clear handwriting and it was signed 'Love, Jane Wilkins, your mother.

The contents of the letter were pretty well much as expected. She was sorry she could not keep me when I was born, I had been on her conscience ever since, she thought about me nearly every day, she had married and had children and grandchildren (she included names and ages), but she would not feel complete until she found me and we could be as one family. I could feel my face redden with anger. 'Tough', I thought. How selfish; it was okay to leave me at the hospital to be given to the children's home for adoption and now when it suited her, she decided she wanted to find me so we could all be 'one happy family'. My first reaction was to tear the letter up and pretend I had never received it but that was not the way to handle it. I went inside, made a mug of tea, returning to the veranda with a notepad and pen to compose my reply. This was to be the first draft which I would hone up and then ask Harry to post it on his return to the UK. I did not want Jane Wilkins to know I was currently on Aspros. I tried to be compassionate but at the same time I needed to be firm so told her I appreciated her circumstances when I was born but as she would have already found out, I never was adopted or fostered and had spent my entire childhood in the home, never knowing what it was like to have parents or be part of a family. It was because of this that I had no desire to be part of her family and as difficult as she may find it I did not want to see her or my half siblings and their children. I concluded by saying that I no longer lived at the address she had sent the letter to and it was best that she did not try to correspond further or try to see me. I resisted the temptation to say the reason I had never been adopted was because I was of mixed parentage; a white mother and an unknown dark skinned father, what was commonly and unkindly referred to in those days as a 'half-cast'. Couples who were prepared to adopt a 'half-cast' were very few and far between.

I was determined not to let the letter get to me but all the same I could not face anything to eat or even a glass of wine before I walked back down the hill to help at the Blue Sea. Once I was at the taverna I found that this week I would be 'meeting and greeting' which involved showing customers to their tables, getting them a drink, taking their food order, keeping them supplied with drinks throughout the evening and finally making up their bill and taking their payment. After my first evening in the kitchen washing up, my role had been keeping the flow of food from kitchen to tables. This new role was just what I needed, as I had little time to think about Jane Wilkin's letter. Before things got busy Anna asked me about Harry and Mike, had they had a good flight and did they like the studio. I told her about the small flight delay, they loved the studio which was so beautifully presented and finally that Mike was in awe of the view from the balcony. I decided, like Georgios, I would greet everyone with 'Καλησπέρα', 'Good evening' and once seated I would ask them 'Τι κανετέ;', 'How are you?' and see how we went from there. I was pleased with the reaction this received; but was it a case that some had eaten at Georgios's taverna and he had taught them some simple phrases or was it a genuine effort to learn a little of the Greek language?

Harry and Mike walked up on Friday evening, arriving about eight. I showed them the house and the garden and introduced them to Rosie before she went off hunting. Harry remarked how well settled I was and they were both impressed with the garden and all the vegetables growing at the back. Earlier in the day I had; marinated some lamb chops and chicken in olive oil, lemon and oregano ready for the barbeque, made a tomato salad, a lettuce salad and cooked some broad beans in olive oil with yoghurt and dill. With these was bread and wine from the shop and to follow some apples which I would slice just before serving and trickle some honey over before sprinkling with cinnamon. We sat out on the veranda sipping ouzos where I told them I had invited a friend who would join us when he had finished work. The friend of course was Bill.

We lit the barbeque just before nine and the coals were starting to glow nicely by the time Bill arrived. Introductions complete and more ouzo's poured, I let Bill do the cooking while Harry and Mike carried the dining table and two additional chairs out onto the veranda. I put the finishing touches to the salads in the kitchen and finally, laid the table. Mike took photos of us grouped round the barbeque and several others of us during the course of the evening. I was a little sceptical about Bill doing the cooking but it appeared he was an old hand at barbequing and everything was cooked perfectly; no charred chops or part cooked chicken. The whole evening was relaxed with us chatting about nothing in particular and as the wine took its hold; laughing at just about everything. The only serious discussion was about car hire which Bill said he would look into first thing in the morning for a three day rental of something cheap and cheerful, starting Sunday. It was nearly one before Bill said he ought to go and get some beauty sleep and shortly after Harry and Mike set off down the hill to Anna's Studios but not before they had stacked all the dishes and plates in the kitchen and carried the table and chairs back inside. I refused all offers with the washing up; this could wait until the morning. As I lay on my bed with the breeze gently blowing through the window, it took some time before sleep overtook my consciousness. I thought about Harry and Mike, both conservatively dressed, they did not draw attention to themselves; I would have hated them to be the victims of homophobia. They looked good together and were obviously very fond of each other. I needed to bear this in mind for when I went back to the UK.

As usual watering the garden took precedence in the morning and I was only just finishing clearing everything away from the previous evening when Harry and Mike turned up. They were on their way to see Bill and stopped by to thank me for yesterday evening. They were quite excited about hiring a car and seeing more of the island and asked if I would like to come with them one day. Very kind but this was their holiday and I did not want to intrude but I did agree to them picking me up on Monday evening and joining them to eat at Sophia's and Aris's taverna, To Klimata, which like the Blue Sea, overlooked the beach. For their final evening we arranged to eat with Bill at Georgios's.

Harry collected me on Monday evening and as he was alone I took the opportunity to tell him about the letter from Jane Wilkins. It was no real secret that I had spent my childhood in a children's home, but I preferred to tell Harry about the letter in private. I had the letter with me so when we pulled up at the back of Anna's Studios I passed it to him to read.
"What you going to do?" he asked "Go and see her when you go back?"
"Nothing of the sort." I replied "I have drafted a letter explaining why, after all these years; I don't want to be part of her family. I have it with me and would really appreciate it, if you would take a look, to make sure I have not been too harsh. I was going to ask you to take it back with you to post in the UK."
I handed him my draft. He read it through twice and with a concerned look said,
"It's absolutely fine Polly but have another think if this is really what you want before you give it to me to post."
I agreed fully knowing that nothing would change my mind but at least it satisfied Harry.

Mike was off the booze that evening; he had one too many the previous evening while they were sat on the balcony after dinner, watching the moonlit sea and listening to the noises of the night. As a result he had been a little fragile during the day and although this had not stopped them going out and about in the car, he felt it was prudent to abstain for at least this one evening. And so a totally alcohol free Mike drove me back home later that evening. He had done most of the talking while we ate; telling me about the places they had discovered in the hire car and he showed me some of the photographs he had taken. A couple of shots he grabbed whilst leaning out of the car window as Harry drove across the mountain road. There were no crash barriers to stop cars driving off the road; if you got it wrong, it was straight down a couple of hundred feet or so into valleys or ravines. He explained, in places it was hair-raising, in particular on tight bends and this was where he took some amazing and clever shots. He was absolutely in awe of the island. Driving me home, his usual effervescent self was replaced by a far more serious Mike.

"Harry was really cut up after we left you at the airport. He has blamed himself for your state of mind. *(Rather a delicate way I thought of putting 'on the verge of a breakdown'.)* I wasn't sure coming here was the right thing to do. I know he still loves you but more as a sister or very good friend, if you understand what I mean. *(Yes, I understood perfectly what he meant.)* I thought it may give him even more guilt feelings but in fact it was the best thing we could have done. After the barbeque at yours he told me on the walk back that he could hardly believe how much you have changed from the person that we had left at the airport at the beginning of May. Seeing you so relaxed and enveloped in your life and the community here in Lionas and of course wanting to see us both has done him the world of good. I think it is because of you that we have been accepted so well here as a couple. Okay we have had a few odd looks and tuts but I believe it is because they know and respect you that we have not been snubbed or stonewalled."

I was not sure how to reply but settled for telling Mike it was good to see them happy together and when I returned, I would try to get out of their hair as soon as possible and set myself up somewhere other than the flat.

The rest of their visit soon passed with our final get together on the Wednesday evening, as planned, at Georgios's where they related to Bill all the 'special' places they had discovered when they had the car and that he was not to reveal them to other visitors otherwise they would no longer be 'special'. I did not accompany them to the airport, instead I waited in the shade of a tree next to Georgios's and as Thanassis came up with them in his taxi he stopped briefly so we could say our goodbyes. It was at this point that I handed Harry the envelope addressed to Jane Wilkins.

"Sure?" asked Harry.

"Absolutely" was my reply.

I waved them off as I watched the taxi disappear up into the village on its journey to the airport.

Chapter 16

Walking back along the track home I thought how I was going to have to give my return to the UK some very careful consideration. Initially I would stay in the flat but in fairness I would have to find somewhere else pretty quickly. I decided, at the end of August to ask Diane to put feelers out for me with the local letting agencies.

I had not been back home long when Eva appeared. Ah, I thought, she would want to know who Harry and Mike were. She had probably heard through the village grapevine but would look to me for verification. I did my best to explain to her in Greek but in the end she looked confused and threw up her arms saying,

"Δεν καταλαβαίνω, απλά δεν καταλαβαίνουν.", "I don't understand, I just don't understand."

Whether it was a case of not understanding or not wanting to understand was debatable, so I told her to sit on the veranda while I poured us a glass each of my homemade lemonade. It did not take long before she calmed down and after about ten minutes, during which she muttered to herself several times, she toddled off down the garden path and back home. I wondered what she would tell all her friends.

That's it, I thought, no more visitors. I can sit back, relax and enjoy my freedom. Just Rosie, me and this dear little house, with its productive garden.

The temperatures rose higher, the ground was bone dry and apart from those flowers that received regular watering there was little or no colour, just dried brown vegetation. Come August all the studios and apartments were full and there was an influx of Athenians who came just once a year to spend a month in their villas. They rarely walked anywhere which meant there were more vehicles driven down to the beach in the mornings and then back up into the hills late afternoon or in the evening.

I am not criticising when I say; they were noisy. After all it is their country, so who am I to say how they should behave. Whenever I passed a taverna you could almost guarantee there would be a table of twelve plus Athenians consuming plate after plate of various different dishes brought out from the kitchens. There were invariably two conversations being conducted at one time; some quite heated. The duration of the meals could last several hours by which time you could sense impatience brewing; the taverna owners and their staff wanted to clear away, either so they could have an afternoon siesta or so they could go home for the night. The children got tetchy either from boredom or tiredness and started running around or they had paddies which invariably ended in tears. The only real competition came from equally noisy parties of Brits who drove round in their Chelsea tractors and who breezed into shops expecting to be given the same class of service they received in Harrods, Fortnum & Mason or the like. But as they say, 'It takes all types to make a world'.

There was no need for me to get involved, apart from helping at the shop and taverna. I could keep myself to myself and the only real annoyance I experienced was from the occasional dust bath as one of the drivers of a 4x4 tried out their off road skills as they passed me on the track. My involvement was about to increase when on the first Friday in August, Anna arrived in the morning while I was hanging out my bed linen on the washing line. She looked both flushed and embarrassed and like everyone else; hot. I offered her a glass of lemonade, which she accepted but instead of us sitting in the cool under the vines above the veranda, she gulped it down, said that was better and then began to tell me about Panos. Bill had told me a bit about Panos; he owned the island's family run car hire company, Hermes Hire Cars and was a cousin of Yiannis. Panos ran the main office in town and Bill rated him highly both as an employer and as a grafter but as Anna explained; Panos had been taken

ill. An ambulance had been called to his office after he had experienced excruciating abdominal pain. In short, he had ignored all the signs of appendicitis, his appendix burst and he had peritonitis. Anna assured me he was going to be okay but instead of having a simple operation to remove his appendix and then return to work quite quickly, the added complication meant he would need a period of convalescence. I looked at Anna quizzically; what had this to do with me, although I had a suspicion as to where this was leading. Anna went on to explain that the family were impressed with the way Bill was running the office here in Lionas and with car hires up by 15% compared to this time last year, they had seconded him to the town office. Panos's two sons would run the office here during their school holidays after which Panos expected to be back working again.   The look of embarrassment returned to Anna's face as she told me the sons, due to other commitments, were not able to cover all the evenings and could I possibly consider running the office on Monday, Tuesdays and Wednesdays between 6-9 p.m. Anna concluded with,

"It's an awful cheek because I know you are already helping Despina and at our taverna but if you don't they are really stuck."

That sounded a bit like emotional blackmail to me. During the following silence I weighed things up. I really did not want any further commitments but then everyone had been so kind and helpful; I could alienate myself by refusing. If I said yes, I would still have Friday, Saturday and Sundays to do as I pleased. In the end I looked Anna straight in the face; she was nervously biting her bottom lip.

"Okay, I'll do it, on two conditions. One, I get full training and don't just get left to get on with it and the second is, I do this without payment. I don't want to become an employee; I am just someone doing somebody else a favour. How does that sound?"

Anna beamed, threw her arms round me and gave me a big hug and a kiss.

"Thank you so much, this will really help tremendously but I know Panos won't let you do this for nothing but I will leave you two to argue that one!"

After another glass of lemonade, this time consumed on the veranda, Anna left me to continue pegging my bed linen on the line. Wednesday was obviously going to be completely full, with most of the day helping Despina in the shop, followed by the car hire office in the evening. In between the two I would have enough time to come home and feed Rosie. I would eat after I had closed the office for the day and no problems with lunch, as Despina always provided this; it was her way of thanking me. She was greatly recovered from her operation both physically and mentally and I suppose she could have managed without me but we got on really well together and being in the shop with her was not like work at all. I think we had a kind of bond, particularly after she found out I had a hysterectomy too. It was something I did not want to talk about but one day when Despina was taking her prescribed hormone replacement tablets I could not help but notice the similarity in packaging to my prescription. I had mine in my bag and pulled the pack out and slid it across the counter where she was sitting. I waited for her reaction. Not quite what I expected; she looked at me pityingly and I realised what she was thinking. Around ten years younger than her, she felt sorry that finality of not being able to have children had come to me so much younger. But I did not want pity, so I told her,

"Δεν είναι ένα πρόβλημα για μένα.", "It is not a problem for me." but I am not sure she believed me.

We hugged each other reassuringly and I think she would probably have ended shedding a few tears had it not been for a customer walking into the shop to pay for a sarong they had picked out from the display outside. I am sure she told Anna but that did not matter, after all it was now one of my lesser hang-ups. Since Amy's visit and announcement she was pregnant I finally appreciated and recognised that whatever thoughts or regret I had since the operation; that motherhood was not for me.

Chapter 17

Back in the UK, Fiona had snapped up Diane's and Tony's offer to buy her half of the business. In the previous Monday's email from Diane, she informed me that the deal would be complete in the next couple of weeks. Fiona, she said, had been a different person and Diane had warmed towards her. Of course Donald taking his own life meant that any life insurance policies he had, would not pay out. And as Fiona had not worked since the birth of their first child it was going to be a big lifestyle change now that she had to support herself and the two children. Fiona had previously worked as a hairdresser and had found a freehold shop with accommodation over it for sale near to Heathrow Airport, in the village of Colnbrook. She was in the process of buying the property with the intention of converting the shop into a hairdressing and beauty salon which she hoped would draw in locals as well as, cabin crew working at the airport. The plan was to use the money from the sale of Donald's half of the business to buy this, move into the flat above and rent the family home. Diane believed Fiona had got her head screwed on financially. If the business took off, Fiona intended to move back to the family home in a couple of years and rent out the flat. Diane concluded the email 'She is a different person, with so much to arrange and organise I think Fiona is enjoying the challenge of making a new life for herself and the kids. I hope she makes a success of it and I have promised to give her advice when it comes to bookkeeping and VAT.' This was good news all round, I did not relish the thought of working with Fiona on my return and I knew Diane and Tony would make excellent business partners and co-directors in the company.

On Saturday morning Bill had arranged to be in the office to show me the 'ins and outs' of car rental. It did not sound too daunting; the hire agreements were all in English and car availability was logged on the computer so it was quick and easy to see what was available for rental and when. There was a safe discreetly located in the small kitchen area where at night; the passports belonging to people who currently had a car out on rental were stored along with any cash deposits, the keys of cars on the forecourt, plus the credit card machine. The buckets, sponges, car shampoo and vacuum were kept in a lock up at the back of the offices. We had two customers come in enquiring about rental for the following week so I had a little hands-on practice using the computer system while Bill guided me through the general procedures. Training complete, Bill looked at me seriously,

"If you get any difficult people, which you won't, then just call across to Petros over at the bar. He said he will keep an eye on you in case there is a problem. So don't forget; just shout and he will be straight over. And one other thing, you're not going to wear shorts, t-shirt and flip flops are you? You'll frighten everyone away!"

Bill could not resist a tease but I could see where he was coming from. I had recently bought a couple of new sundresses, lightweight cardigans and sandals for working with Despina and at the Blue Sea so I assured him I would do my best not to scare customers and I would put on a bit of slap too, to make myself presentable! With that, Panos's eldest son, Spiros arrived on his scooter ready to take over for the morning. Between sixteen and seventeen years old I thought he might be a little resentful having to give up his holidays to help in the family business but if he was, he didn't show it. We shook hands and I asked after Panos. He told me he was out of hospital and laughed before saying his father was driving his mother crazy; he was not a good patient. Spiros would run the office most mornings and his younger brother Maichail would take over in the afternoons; they would take it in turn with the evening shifts. He thanked me profusely for helping and the family would not hear of me working for nothing. After I had closed down the office, I was to go to Georgios's to eat, I was to choose whatever I wanted off the menu and if I wanted the most expensive bottle of wine, then I was to order it. I tried to refuse by saying it was my pleasure to help but he insisted and if I had said anymore I would risk offending him by turning down their generosity. It is the way Greeks are.

I enjoyed working in the office. Between six and eight proved to be a busy time when couples, who were on their way out to eat, came into the office either to book a vehicle or to enquire about availability and prices. I was able to tell them about various places on the island that may interest them; secluded beaches, ruined villages, monasteries, mountain passes etc. Between eight and nine it was quieter and gave me time to valet the cars returned earlier so they were ready to go out again the following morning. It was while I was washing a Fiat Panda that two guys approached. They were pretty well tanked up.

"Hi there doll." said the tallest and fattest of the two, "Got a 4x4 we can rent? Me and Ray here want to get out on the rough and go up the mountain and we wanna go somewhere where there are some babes. Only there ain't no babes here, except for the odd travel rep and yourself of course." he laughed.

I had already been primed by Bill that even if there were no cars out on rental that the answer to these types was 'No, all our cars are booked.' I put the sponge back in the bucket.

"I'll just check for you." I replied. "Did you have any particular days in mind?"

"Nope", said Ray "We just wanna get away from this place, nothing's going on."

Well, I thought to myself, if you had done your homework first you would have realised this resort is for couples and young families and you should have gone to a livelier island. They followed me into the office. Ray slumped in one of the chairs with his leg over one arm, while his mate perched on the corner of my desk. Ray's mate leaned over towards me breathing beer in my face, the smell of this mixed with suntan lotion was almost nauseating.

"I am sorry, but you are blocking the light from the screen. Would you sit in the chair next to Ray, please."

Ray laughed, "She don't fancy you Dan. She don't know a good man that's the trouble Ray. What's your name doll and what time do you finish? We can wait for you over the road and go out as a threesome. You know what I mean?" he leered at me.

I kept my cool, "Well I am afraid we are completely fully booked for the next week, that's not just 4x4's, we don't have any cars available, not even a small one like the Panda on the forecourt. If you'll excuse me, I have to finish washing the car outside ready for tomorrow."

Ray looked agitated, he put his leg down and leant across the desk "No", he shouted in my face, "We won't excuse you. You didn't answer me mate's question. He asked you your name and what time you finish? If you don't tell us, we're going to sit over the road and wait and wait until you do finish, ain't we Dan?"

Dan nodded and leered at me. Keep calm, I told myself and don't let them see your hands shaking.

"Well, I think that's a very good idea." I replied "You go and sit over the road while I finish the car and then we'll go and see if we can find some action shall we?" My heart was up in my throat as I spoke, "Come on lads, let's go outside."

"Things is looking up." Ray winked to Dan "Gotta a bit of taste this one, reckon we gonna be all right here."

I walked through the office door with them in tow and once outside, I filled my lungs with the warm evening air and shouted "Petros" as loud as I could. The result was instantaneous. Petros came running from inside the bar, he never stopped to check the road for vehicles, and in hot pursuit was Jacques, the French student who was working during University summer vacation. Their instant reactions had an immediate effect on Dan and Ray, who suddenly sobered up. Dan was the first to speak.

"Hey we don't mean no harm just inviting the lady out for a drink."

"Yeh, that's right." piped up Ray, "Don't want no trouble."

Ignoring their comments, Petros and Jacques frog marched them over the road and inside the bar while I retreated back inside the office. I sat behind the desk with my head in my hands. My entire body was shaking with shock. A few minutes later, Petros walked in, picked up my cardigan from the back of the chair and put it round my shoulders. In front of me he placed a glass of Metaxas brandy.

"Here" he said "Drink this, it will help steady you. And don't you worry; there will be no more trouble from those two. I promise you. When you have finished here and eaten, come back to the bar. I can see you are shaken; Jacques will walk you home."

All I could manage in reply was to look up into his eyes and say. "Oh, thank you Petros."

I slowly sipped the brandy with the last of the coffee in the filter jug, had a cry and began to feel calmer. I returned to cleaning the car, put away the keys and credit card machine in the safe, washed up the coffee jug, filter, coffee cups and brandy glass and finally turned the key in the office door. Petros was standing by the bar door as I walked over with the glass. There were concerned looks from those who had witnessed the whole affair; I gave them a somewhat forced smile to show all was well.

"Okay?" asked Petros.

"Yes much better now thank you. I can't thank you and Jacques enough. I was so scared."

"No problem but don't forget, there will be no more trouble from those two. Jacques and I have seen to that. Now you go off and have dinner and whenever you are ready come back, have another brandy and Jacques will walk you home."

"Thanks", I said, handing him the glass and giving him a reassuring smile.

What Petros and Jacques had done and said I never knew but I did see Dan and Ray passing the office again during the period of their holiday. They walked purposefully along the road with their eyes straight ahead looking neither towards the office or Petros's bar. They never came back to talk about hiring a 4x4.

I sat at my usual table on the veranda in Georgios's taverna. He sensed all was not well, so I told him briefly of my experience. I had lost my appetite but Georgios managed to tempt me with stifado (chunks of meat cooked in a rich sauce) and lemon potatoes. While I waited, I sipped a glass of wine and went back over in my mind what had happened. Had I over reacted? Had I misinterpreted a bit of holiday fun for a real threat? Should I have just walked over to Petros and asked for help? If I had tried to deal with the situation myself, what would have happened? Ah, so many questions. By the time Georgios served my meal, I had decided there was no point trying to answer these questions, I had reacted as I felt the situation warranted and now I needed a diversion to stop me dwelling on the whole affair. The stifado was quite delicious, with the sauce flavoured with cinnamon, cumin and paprika. I would have to ask in the kitchen for the rest of the ingredients so that once the temperatures cooled in September and before I returned to the UK, I could cook the dish at home. The potatoes were perfect, cooked slowly in the oven with olive oil plus some water to provide steam. When they were soft they were removed from the oven, lemon squeezed over and kept warm ready to serve.

I caught Georgios's eye, "Πολύ καλά.", "Very good." I told him, "Τέλεια", "Perfect"   He gave a bow in recognition of my complement.

Diversion came in the form of a couple who had engaged in conversation a couple of times over my garden gate and who introduced themselves as Joy and Barry. In their late forties, they told me how they enjoyed walking and preferred not to lie in the sun all day. I had given them a couple of tips and as they were going to rent a car, I suggested a particularly picturesque village to visit and walking up the mountain. Walking up the mountain in August was not as daft as it sounded. There was a well-defined dirt road, cut so that if there was a fire in the forest, tenders could easily access the area. Sheltered by overhanging trees, the track was shady throughout the day. I told them, the view at the top down to Lionas and neighbouring villages was spectacular as was the vista across the sea to other islands. Anyway, they walked in and sat at the table next to me. They were both florid and rather short of breath. Once they had regained their composure, Joy explained they had been for a circular walk and completely misjudged the timing and as it was nearly ten, did I think they were too late to get anything to eat. I told them I didn't think there would be any problem but just in case they had started to clean the grills, the staff would probably appreciate it if they chose a pre-cooked dish. The stifado is delicious, I added, pointing to my plate. They placed their order, the stifado with rice; by then the lemon potatoes were sold out. As they started to relate what they had been doing over the past few days, I suggested they joined me so we could converse with ease. It was their first visit to the island and I picked up on their excitement; it was just the same as my first visit with Amy. They were collecting their hire car in the morning, a Panda; probably the one I had been valeting that evening, which they felt would be ideal for negotiating some of the twisting mountain roads. I agreed this was an excellent choice. When we had finished eating, I asked them if they would like to join me for a Metaxa at Petros's bar and together with coffees we sat and enjoyed the end of what could have been for me, a traumatic evening. Barry insisted on paying, as a thank you for recommending places to go in the car, but Petros refused to take any money.

He explained, "Polly had a little upset earlier this evening and you have made her smile again, so this is my thank you to you."

We all thanked Petros for his generosity and thank goodness, Joy and Barry made no enquiries as to what the 'little upset' had entailed. They were staying at the Golden Sun and walked back with me, leaving Jacques free to clear tables and close down for the evening. As we walked along the dusty road Joy asked how long I had left on the island. It was about two months before I would return to the UK, it was going to be difficult to leave, I had been made so welcome and tonight was a prime example of how I was regarded but as I said to Joy, all good things must come to an end.

Chapter 18

Word travels fast in a small Greek village and Bill came round to see me in the morning before he drove to work. I assured him I was fine and would be back in the office that evening.

"Maybe, I should have told you to wear your usual shorts and t-shirt." he grinned before continuing softly, "Who could blame any man for fancying you, with your soft brown skin and shiny brown hair."

Now what was he trying to say, was he complimenting me or what? I put my hands in my shorts pockets, tilted my hips to one side and smirked.

"You'd better get off to work. See you Thursday morning."

He smiled, turned and walked up the path stopping to blow me a friendly kiss at the garden gate. As he drove down the track, I thought what a good friend I had in Bill. Hopefully, when the bulk of the visitors had gone home, Panos was back at work and the weather was a bit cooler maybe we could squeeze in some more time together before we both went our separate ways.

Later in the month a padded envelope arrived for me in the post. Amy and Harry had brought my post out in June and July and the envelope contained the latest batch of mail. Nothing very exciting, just a couple of bank statements and some statutory documents to sign and a return in connection with the changes in company directors. There was little else of note apart from a handwritten envelope. Written in a different hand to the one from Jane Wilkins; I opened it with a sense of foreboding. Sitting down at the table, I slowly unfolded the notepaper to reveal a family snapshot. Written on the back was each individuals name with their relationship to Jane Wilkins in brackets. I studied the photograph, particularly Jane Wilkins who was in the centre of the group. These people meant nothing to me. The letter was from her son, Mark, who very politely thanked me for replying to his mother's letter.   He went on to say that she fully understood how I felt but he was asking me to reconsider. He hoped that by seeing a photograph of the family, my family, taken the previous Christmas I would consider joining them for this year's Christmas festivities. Oh dear, I thought, do you really mean this Mark, have you considered what the introduction of another sibling to the family could mean, have you considered John, Jane's husband, how he would feel. No I think not. From his tone in the letter, I could tell Mark thought the world of his mother. It seemed to me; he was thinking of her, doing what he thought what was best for her, without him reasoning things through properly. I had no desire to meet the people in the photograph but I could not say so to Mark. Instead I replied with a photograph of myself, which I asked Bill to take on my camera. I posed on a dry stone wall at the back of the garden, with the olive trees and mountain in the background. The result looked like a typical holiday snap. I had the photo printed in town and in my letter to Mark I acknowledged his request for me to reconsider which for his benefit I said I had done. However, I was not changing my mind but had enclosed a photograph of myself taken on a recent holiday (bit of a lie there). This was for him to either keep for himself or give to his mother or just discard it. I repeated that I had moved and suggested that he should not correspond further as there was no guarantee that the new occupants would continue to forward mail (another bit of a lie). I sent the addressed envelope to Harry with an explanation and asked him to stamp and post if for me. What would I do with the two letters and the family photograph? Keep them I suppose. Sometime in later years I may want to remind myself of my family; the family I chose never to meet.

In August the temperatures topped 40°C on the beach which resulted in those who insisted on staying out in the midday sun, getting sunstroke. This reminded me of the old Noël Coward song in which the lyrics say, 'Mad dogs and Englishmen go out in the midday sun.' I had tomatoes in abundance and if I had tried to keep pace with them I would have spent a good amount of time each day on the loo! I gave some to Eva and told her, if there were too many to give them to her friends. In return she gave me eggs from her friend's chickens which made wonderful deep golden coloured omelettes. I chopped up pieces of salami and feta cheese and added these while the eggs were cooking in the pan and popped the open omelette under the grill rather than try turning it over. I ate this with a salad and some crusty bread. I had no qualms about the amount of salt the salami and feta added to my diet. I lost a lot of salt through perspiration and needed to replenish my body's stocks. I drank copious amounts of bottled water; I always carried a small bottle with me and a large one in a rucksack when out walking. Rosie coped well with the heat; cats have such inner born sense and she always found a cool shady place to sleep and often shared my omelettes or meat from the barbeque. She was a sheer delight to have around and at times a cause for anxiety when she broke routine and failed to turn up for her food. I contemplated as to what she would do when I went back to the UK and took masses of photographs of her to look back on in years to come. I also took photographs of the garden, the house (inside and out), the lane outside and well just about everything, including the churchyard on the outskirts of the village.

Bill ate with me on Friday and Saturday evenings. It was usually dark by the time he arrived but the lamps and candles provided sufficient light for us to cook on the barbeque and then to eat by. He related stories and experiences from Australia and I in turn told him a bit about my life and the laughs Amy and I had enjoyed during the years of our friendship. When he left, which was usually well past midnight, he always took my hand and kissed it, thanking me for dinner even though he was the one who did the barbequing.

By late August the general decline in temperature became quite noticeable. It was still in the high twenties and thirties but the heat was nowhere near as oppressive. At the end of August the Athenians returned to the city and the owners of the Chelsea tractors returned to their homes for another year. When they left, the village was quieter, even though the accommodations remained full and there was still a steady flow of tourists coming and going each Thursday. Diane had contacted the letting agencies for me who emailed a selection of suitable properties for rent. Those of interest and assuming they were still available, I could view on my return.

Early September I started to see the return of familiar faces; those who holidayed on the island twice a year, in May and again in September. They wanted to know how hot the summer had been and delighted in visiting shops, bars and tavernas to find out how everyone was and when they left, they did so with promises of, 'See you next year.' That excluded me of course because in just a few weeks, I too would be leaving Aspros. I decided not to think too much about leaving until a fortnight before my flight. That would leave plenty of time to run the store cupboards down, throw away what I did not want to take back with me and say my 'goodbyes'.

Mid-September the schools started back and the music evenings at the Blue Sea finished at the same time. Although I knew the taverna would not be so busy, I offered to continue helping on Thursday evenings. I liked being involved and although Yiannis said they would be fine and that I should make the most of my last few weeks and go and enjoy myself, Anna threw a scornful glance at Yiannis and jumped at my offer. Afterwards she told me that the boys would still help on Fridays and the weekend until the taverna closed at the end of September but that she would have to cover the other evenings, so with my offer she would only have to work on Monday, Tuesday and Wednesday evenings.

Everything was winding down. The shelves in the tourist supermarkets became destocked of tinned and packaged products. There still remained regular supplies of fresh produce but because they tended to run out quite quickly, it was always best to buy milk in the morning. The small shop near the square which supplied the locals still had full shelves but for me this involved a walk back up the hill carrying bags. It was all really rather sad. The weather would remain pleasant for some weeks to come but the tour operators could not guarantee filling planes and the accommodations and so stopped offering Aspros as a destination soon after the first week in October. This would, of course, not stop those who made their own travel arrangements but when the charter flights ceased it meant a plane to Athens followed by either an internal flight or a ferry to get to Aspros. Despina told me it was not worth keeping the shop or the studios open and they and most others would be closing. It was only walkers who tended to visit in October and they normally made their accommodation reservations before they arrived and were happy to either eat in the local's taverna in the village or buy from the village shop and cook in their studios, apartments or villas.

During the third week in September, while taking an early evening walk, I stopped to talk to Stavros who was working his vegetable plot. I told him I would be drawing out the money to pay him cash for the rent the following week and asked him who would be taking over Maria's house when I went home. He just lifted his shoulders, held his hands out and said,

"No one. When you go home Polly my mother's house will be empty again. You have looked after it so well these past months, my mother would have appreciated that. You know, you can always rent it again next summer, if you want." he said half-jokingly.

"I may take you up on that." I replied, forcing a smile to hide the sadness I felt that the dear little house that had been my home over the past months, would be without anyone to clean it, to sit on its veranda or to tend its garden.

He gave me some carrots he had promised Eva which I said I would drop off on my way back. I carried on walking down the dusty track that eventually led down to the beach. I walked slowly without purpose, swinging the bag of carrots and kicking the dust with my sandals. I dwelled on the thought of Maria's house being empty and the garden growing with weeds and about returning to the UK when my day to day routine would be governed by work and the business. I also thought about the freedom I would lose; freedom I had so enjoyed over the past months. By the time I reached the beach, my mind was in turmoil. I sat on a tussock at the back of the beach for a while. I had a decision to make. I drew a '+' and a '-' next to each other in the sand and then proceeded to write, as best as you can in sand, under each one. With the facts in front of me, the decision was easy. I picked up the bag of carrots and turned back up the track, this time walking with purpose. At the allotments, I stopped again to talk to Stavros and when I carried on back towards Eva's and home my heart was light; the sadness had lifted.

When I came to the garden gate, I stood in silence and let my eyes run round the garden, across the veranda up the walls and onto the roof. I didn't go in but smiled and carried on to see Bill. He was busy, on the phone arranging a car for a lady who was sat in front of his desk. A couple were lingering in the background, obviously waiting to speak to Bill, so I gave him a wink and gestured I would wait at Petros's bar, over the road. I ordered a frappé and sat at a table near the roadside. It was about three quarters of an hour before Bill was free during which time I had several short conversations with locals and passing tourists. Bill wandered over; he looked tired, it had been a busy season with long hours, particularly during August. He bent over and kissed my cheek before sitting down next to me.

"Not quite time to shut up shop" he commented "but I could do with a bit of fresh air and I can keep my eyes on things from over here. I fancy a beer but until I close up for the night, a frappé will have to do."

He ordered a frappé for himself and a glass of white wine for me. He looked at me quizzically.

"Come on then, I can see you have something on your mind; let's have it."

"Well", I started, "you know you asked me if I could stay a bit longer, rather than fly back on the 10th, so we could have some time exploring the island together before you go back. It's sorted; I am cashing in my ticket. Instead, and because the flights off the island are only twice a week later in the month, I am going to book the ferry to Piraeus on the 20th, stay overnight and then fly from Athens to Heathrow on the 21st."

I felt my face flush, which I hoped he would interpret as one of pleasure of spending time together without the hassle of work commitments for him and for me, helping Despina and Anna and not that I was bending the truth. Bill beamed, slapped a hand down on the table.

"Bloody fantastic!" he exclaimed.

He put down his frappé, stood up and headed back to the office, calling over his shoulder that he was going to call Panos straight away and ask him if he could have a car for at least a few days. While I waited for his return, something inside me niggled; why on earth did I not tell him the truth. I know I wanted to keep my secret, the secret only known to Stavros but at the same the niggle reminded me that lies always catch up with you. Bill was still beaming when he walked back across the road.

"Seems he was going to give me a bonus when I finished, says I have done wonders for the business here and could not have done without me when he was in hospital and he wants me back next year. But he said, instead of money, I could have a car for a week. Nothing flashy; just a little run-a-round. So looks as though we have got something to celebrate. How about, after I shut up the office, we go and eat at Georgios's."

I looked at my watch, "While you shut up, I'll go back and feed Rosie and put something a bit more presentable on."

"By all means, feed the cat but stay as you are; I quite like my women scruffy." he laughed and almost immediately realised his mistake. "Oh no, I meant; I quite like my friends scruffy."

I was just about to stand up and shout 'I AM NOT YOUR WOMAN AND DON'T YOU FORGET IT.' when I thought what the heck, just a slip of the tongue, why spoil our friendship, after all he knows how the land lies between us; he had never tried to push our relationship beyond friendship. Instead I stood up, looked down into his eyes, smiled, pointed a finger on his chest and said,

"Like it or not this girl is going home to put on a bit of slap and a dress! See you in about three-quarters of an hour then?"

A look of relief came over his face. "Spot on." he replied.

Chapter 19

I had already checked with the bank that I could draw out the rent money in cash for Stavros, plus of course there was that bit extra for Yiannis. So when I went into town the following week there were no problems at the counter. The teller obligingly counted out the notes in front of me before splitting the two amounts and putting them into separate sealed plastic bags and then into a brown envelope. Before going to the bank I checked my emails at the internet café. All was well at the office and Amy updated me on her pregnancy and the family in general. I had already drafted the basics of my replies to them, plus one to Harry, at home so it was just a case of bashing these out on the keyboard ready to send. I hesitated with each message before I hit the send button. I now had a whole week before I was back in town, when I would read their responses. In the meantime I could only speculate what their reactions would be.

I wasted no time handing over the rent money. On my walk from the bus stop down through the village, I stopped off at the shop so I could pay Stavros. The shelves and racks were looking a little sparse but this was good news as they had obviously had a good season and were left with minimal stock to pack away and store. I gave Stavros my rent money; he didn't even bother to count it, he just rolled the notes and put them in his top pocket. I stayed for a coffee and while we drank the strong brew between sips of chilled water, Despina told me how she was going to miss me and asked if I would come back and visit next year. Good old Stavros, I thought, he has kept the secret, hasn't even told his dear wife. I told Despina that I really hoped to return early summer at which her face lit up. She told me that I must phone her when I had a date and then she would spread the news around the village. Coffees finished, it was time to go home and as I said farewell and walked out of the shop, Stavros followed me.   He put his hand on my shoulder,

"Are you sure Polly?" he enquired.

"Yes absolutely." I replied.

The truthful reply should have been – 'Yes, I think so.'

I decided I would walk down to the beach in the afternoon.   As Yiannis would be almost sure to be preparing dishes for the evening, I could pop into the taverna and give him his money. First of all, I would go home and have the tiropita I had bought in town, for my lunch. I had not been indoors for more than a few minutes before my mobile rang. It was Amy; I was not going to have to wait until next week for a response to my email. What followed was a veritable tirade. She was fuming and ranted about me having had too much sun and losing my head, had I really thought it out and, rather sarcastically, wasn't I being just a 'bit' selfish and what about the office and Harry; had I thought about them. After she had finished and it was my turn to speak, for a moment I couldn't think how to start. I needed to be truthful and sound positive

"It's quite simple Amy." I started "I don't want to come back, not just yet anyway. I have given it serious thought, I need more time; I am not ready to face the rigours of work. I am not being selfish; honest. I have sent an email to Harry that basically gives him the option of carrying on with the flat as we are or for him or Mike to buy out my share or to sell it so they can buy a place of their own. I also told him I was happy to start with divorce proceedings, amicably of course. As for the office, you are my best friend so I am trusting you not tell anyone else Amy. I am going to become what is in effect a sleeping partner until I return next spring. I will keep my shares and directorship but will take only a nominal salary; just enough to preserve my state pension. I still expect to be kept abreast of the finances with regular monthly reports."

It was Amy's turn to go quiet.

"Well" she started, "you really have thought things through. I don't know what to say, except I am sorry for my outburst. I should have realised you wouldn't do *anything* without covering *everything*. But I am going to miss you, you know, especially when I pop in December."

I could tell she was almost in tears, so I assured her I would miss her too but I was going to get a laptop and we could email more often and she could send me baby photographs to keep me up to date. By the time we had finished we were laughing and would have carried on chatting a lot longer had it not been for Amy needing to get ready for the school run.

The one question Amy had not asked and that was how I would manage financially. This was no problem, even though I had been drawing a reduced salary during my absence from the business. The reduction was commensurate with me no longer being in the office on a day to day basis but allowing for my advice and knowledge of the business. I had in fact been more like a consultant. The reduced salary had been more than enough to keep me here on Aspros and keep up with my half of the mortgage payments on the flat. I still had plenty to keep me going for several more months, plus I had savings and then there would be the money coming from my share of the flat. I planned to invest the money from the flat sale so I would have a lump sum behind me when I returned to the UK but if I needed a little extra, I would have this to fall back on.

Following Amy's phone call, I took my swimming costume, towel, sun cream and a bottle of water in my rucksack down to the beach. Yiannis was busy preparing papousakia when I arrived at the Blue Sea. He was singing to the music on the radio and was in extremely good spirits.

"It's been a good year." he told me "The studios have been full and the taverna has been so busy, some nights I have had to turn people away." he laughed "But I am glad we will close at the end of the week. I need a rest and so does Anna. She is such a good worker and mother; I don't know what I would do without her help. Of course she complains from time to time but that is only when she is particularly stressed out with all the work or if the children are playing her up."

I handed him the cash, saying this was what I owed him but he would have none of it.

"I cannot take this after all the help you have given us here at the taverna. No, you keep it, put it towards your visit to come and see us next year. You will come back won't you?"

I knew it was pointless arguing about the money, if I had it would have caused offence, instead I told him I would do just that as I certainly planned to holiday here next year.

The beach was perfect; golden sands backed by the gardens and a few tavernas, holiday homes and lets. The sun was still strong during the late morning through to the late afternoon but had lost the extreme heat of July and August. Due to my parentage, my skin was a natural golden brown but I still needed to take care and my visits to the beach during July and August had been fairly infrequent. This was not entirely due to the intensity of the sun but also down to the numbers of people. Such a beautiful beach it attracted visitors and locals from miles around and as I found; it could get very busy. There was a constant flow of vehicles going down in the morning with a quiet period from midday until the late afternoon when, except those staying to eat at one of the beachside tavernas, they all made their way back up the narrow twisting road. But now it was perfect and I enjoyed a dip in the sea, floating on my back with the blue skies and just a few wispy white clouds above and small fishes swimming in the azure sea beneath me. No wonder I did not want to leave Aspros. Of course, I appreciated it would not be like this throughout the year and I wondered when I should relieve Stavros of the secret he shared with me and tell everyone I was staying on. After a few minutes contemplation, I decided to stick to my original plan and wait until Bill had gone back to Australia before I broke the news. Initially I would tell Despina, Anna and Eva who would no doubt spread the word around and then take it from there.

Chapter 20

The emails back from Diane and Harry were pretty well much as I expected. From what they said, I deduced Amy had spoken to them after her phone call to me. All the same they expressed concerns as to how I would manage over the winter months. Diane had consulted Tony about my 'sleeping partner' arrangement and both were in agreement. Harry's email was quite long and detailed but basically boiled down to yes, he would contact his solicitor and discuss divorce proceedings. With regard to the flat, they had given this some serious thought and decided the best way forward was to sell it and buy a place of their own. Apparently, after visiting some friends who had a mews style property with a small manageable courtyard garden, Mike had been hankering for something similar. As long as I was not in a hurry to release my share of the flat, Harry said they would start looking and when they found something would put the flat on the market. There was always a demand for flats in the area and he was sure they would soon find a buyer, preferably one who did not have a property to sell. He asked me to consider what I would like to do with all my 'stuff' that I had left behind. On the nearby commercial estate there was a warehouse that offered storage units of varying sizes and he said he could, if I wanted, move it there.

There was an email from Amy apologising again for her outburst on the phone and asking me if I would consider coming back for Christmas. This was so I could see the new baby and join in their family celebrations. She had spoken to her mum & dad and they said I was more than welcome to stay with them. This gave me something to think about. The idea of going back for Christmas appealed but I was not so sure about staying with Amy's parents, especially as her mum tolerated me rather than actually liking and approving of me. Maybe it was because Amy was conventional, getting married and having a family, whereas I had been the business woman with a string of relationships before I married Harry. I also thought she was a little prejudiced because of my parentage. Of course, if I did go back this would be an ideal opportunity to go through my things at the flat and put what I wanted to keep long term into storage.

I was quite excited at the prospect of seeing more of the island with Bill. We spent a couple of evenings, sat on my veranda, pouring over a map of the island deciding where we would go. Top of our list was Aspros's one and only mountain, Mount Nosia, which stands just over 1600 metres high. We decided we would go on the first really clear day, this way we could pretty well guarantee good views when we got to the top. Closing our eyes and pointing a finger on the map, decided a couple of places; we had absolutely no idea what these would be like. We had the use of the car from Friday 11th. The 10th was the last day for charter flights off the island and with all the cars booked to come back on Wednesday this would leave Thursday completely clear for Bill to finalise the paperwork, clean the office and valet the insides of the cars. It was pointless washing the exteriors as they were to go into storage and would get filthy over the winter months. Finally he would drive to the main office on Friday with the computer and papers to hand over to Panos and collect our run-a-round for the following week.

As soon as the last transfer coach left Lionas on the 10th for the airport, the village felt empty and quiet. Some of the bars and tavernas had already closed and those that had remained open wasted no time in cleaning kitchens, stacking chairs and tables inside, taking down awnings, cutting vines that had provided shade in the summer months, before the doors were finally shut and locked. It was similar with studios and apartments where bed linen was washed and stored in plastic bags, beds were upended and mattresses moved to one room and propped up against a wall. Crockery etc. was left in the cupboards and would be given a clean before opening next year. The seasonal staff that waited tables had already gone home and I had said farewell a couple of days ago to Jacques who along with Petros had come to my assistance, when I had a problem with tourists, Ray and Don. On the Wednesday morning, I helped Despina pack away the remaining stock in the shop while Stavros went off to shut up a couple of the villas he looked after. At times, Despina was nearly in tears. She said she was going to miss me and thanked me time and time again for the help and support I had given her both personally and in the shop.

It all felt sad. I imagined there would be a massive village party at the weekend, one that would celebrate the success of the season and give friends and family, who had little time for socialising over the past months, an opportunity to come to together and relax. But I was wrong. After working so many hours over the summer months, with sleep grabbed at odd hours and sometimes in odd places, all everyone wanted to do was to finish up and sleep.

I went with Bill on the Friday afternoon into town to the Hermes main office. Panos greeted us with a smile and firm handshake before Bill handed over the final paperwork, computer and the keys to the office and cars. Panos said, he and his sons would collect the cars over the weekend and bring them to the compound on the edge of town. Now all that was left was for Panos to hand Bill his final pay and for us to find out what sort of car we would have for the following week. We had driven into town in one of the Suzuki Jimnys and quite expected to be changing this for a more modest Fiat Panda or Daewoo Matiz but when Bill went to hand over the Jimny keys, Panos told him this was our vehicle for the week.

"Go off", he said throwing his arms up in the air, "and explore some of the rougher dirt roads. Go and find the traditional old villages of Aspros and some secluded bays to swim in. When you have finished, park the Jimny outside the office and put the keys through the letterbox."

We both thanked Panos for his generosity but he insisted the thanks were all his, to Bill for running the main office and to me for helping to man the Lionas office after his operation.

Bill insisted that the first place we should go to was the port at Gemara, this was so I would know exactly where to go a week Sunday. I felt such a fraud pretending to be interested in where the ticket office was. I was just thankful Bill did not suggest I bought a ticket in advance. The town was busy and with the shops just opened after siesta, the streets were bustling with activity. There were a few hotels on the front providing accommodation for those in transit between ferries. These were quite bland, functional and served their purpose. We stopped at a harbour side café for a frappé, sitting outside on cane chairs with their bright soft cushions. We spent quite a bit of time here people watching before I suggested we bought some meat to barbeque back at my house. Just four shops up the first side street there was a traditional butcher displaying whole carcasses above trays of joints and chops etc. We settled for some lamb cutlets, these were small and relatively fat free. I got an extra one as a treat for Rosie. As we walked back to the Jimny I dipped into a bakers for a loaf of bread.

Now the last charter flight had left the island, the owners of the studios where Bill had been staying understandably wanted to close their accommodation. Fortunately Stavros had been only too pleased to offer him one of his studios which were in the small block next to their shop and house. Bill had moved his gear there the previous evening and was quite delighted when he discovered how well fitted and roomy it was, plus there was a balcony with a view of the sea. We dropped the Jimny off outside the studios just before 7 p.m. and walked back to my house in the fast fading light. It was like walking through a ghost town or one of those wild west towns you see in films where there is no-one to be seen. All Lionas lacked was tumbleweed blowing down the centre of the road! I began to have misgivings as to whether I was going to last the winter here but assured myself, if it didn't work I was under no obligation to stay.

The evenings had a definite chill now but the warmth generated by the barbeque took off the edge. Wearing long trousers and fleeces we were able to sit out and eat our barbequed lamb cutlets, peppers and courgettes plus olive oil soaked bread accompanied by a bottle of retsina, with just the company of the stars and Rosie, of course. We revised our plans for the next week deciding against some of the places we had been to before. Instead we incorporated some of the more remote mountain villages we would be able to access with the Jimny. After we had cleared away and drunk our coffees with a glass of Metaxa brandy we decided to go up the mountain the following day. I would make a picnic to take with us and Bill said he would collect me about 9.30 a.m.

All went according to plan; the following day was bright and remained so throughout our drive up to the car park, which doubled as a picnic area. This was about two-thirds of the way up the mountain and from here we walked on the continuing track to the top of Nosia. The views were magnificent and we spent time just standing looking down on Lionas and the surrounding villages and countryside. I took a number of photographs which I knew would not do the view justice but at least they would be better than nothing.

"Bloody beautiful." gasped Bill "How privileged we have been living down there these past months. Look, I can see the ruined monastery." he said, excitedly tracing his finger along the path from the village towards its crumbling remains.

"Aw Polly, just think of the all the breakfasts we have enjoyed there. We're going to have to make our last one next Thursday a real special one."

I agreed, while at the same time I was thinking of all the times I would be able to walk there during the months while Bill was back in Australia and how I would see the changing of the seasons and he wouldn't.

The next couple of days can only be termed as brilliant. We went to some fantastic places; sometimes we just parked the Jimny in the middle of nowhere and walked for miles. We stopped by a hillside village, left in ruins by the last major earthquake and let our imaginations run riot as to how life would have been when it had been a thriving community. We looked at faded shop signs, fig trees growing up through roofs and doors hanging off their hinges as we walked up the still recognisable cobbled streets. It was tranquil and not the slightest bit eerie. Stopping at roadside tavernas we ate some truly wonderful flavoursome dishes in the company of inquisitive locals. Surely we were tourists and why had we not gone home last week with the rest? Between us we managed to explain but I hated telling the lie that I was going home on Sunday.

I was feeling more deceitful and dishonest as each day passed. It was starting to play on my mind, that I had not shared my secret with Bill; instead telling him a lie about going home. We had been having such a great time together and now I was finding making conversation a strain. It all came to a head when we were sat above a bay; a curve of blue seas and golden sands. We were contemplating whether to follow the goat tracks down or whether it would prove too steep when Bill said,

"Your hearts not in this is it? Something's on your mind, you are too quiet. Come on out with it."

What could I do, I had to tell him, I could not pretend everything was all right. In the long run that would just make matters worse. I took a deep breath and out it came,

"I'm so so sorry I have not been honest, I've told you a lie."

I felt tears welling up so another good deep breath and,

"I am not going back on Sunday." I blurted and hung my head in shame, waiting for his reaction.

What I expected his reaction to be I don't know but not this. There was a pause before he said loudly,

"That explains it." I was aware that Bill was turning towards me. "Look up at me." he ordered.

I did as I was told. I could tell my face was flushed with embarrassment. He looked me in the eyes.

"You see, the other day I saw Stavros was offloading some new heaters. They were all boxed and he was putting them in the shop. I commented about him buying them for the house before the winter set in. But he replied they had oil heating and they were for your house. He immediately looked awkward and changed the subject by asking if the studio was okay and if I needed anything to just come and knock on the door. Now if he was re-letting after you left, surely he would refer to it as his mother's, Maria's house, so that made me suspicious. But why didn't you tell me Polly? Why did you lie to me? Who else knows? Is it just me who you kept in the dark? Just look at the state you have worked yourself up into."

By the time he had finished, I was in tears. Of course it was silly of me and I could not think of a good reason why I had lied. All I could say between sobs was,

"I didn't want you to try to make me change my mind. The only one on the island who knows is Stavros; I was going to start spreading the word around when you had left and then email you when you got home. It seemed the best way but it all sounds so stupid now."

I thought he would be really mad at me but instead he half-smiled and said quietly,

"Well it's out now. I'll keep it to myself. No point in letting it spoil our, I mean *my* last few days."

Neither of us felt like trying the goat path and we were both a little subdued. We drove back pretty well much in silence, only punctuated by me giving directions. Bill stopped outside my house and I was prepared for the worse.

"Out you get." he ordered. "I'll take the Jimny up to the studio and then I'll meet you at the corner in what, say about an hour? We'll walk down to the village to the kafenion; we could both do with a drink and we'll round off the day with dinner in the taverna."

I was so ashamed of myself; all I could muster was,

"Thank you." as I climbed out of the Jimny, like a child who knows they have done wrong.

Rosie was waiting for me with a welcoming meow. I stroked her behind her ears and she rolled over for me to tickle her tummy.

"Oh Rosie, that was a bad thing I did." and more tears rolled down my cheeks.

The hour gave me enough time to feed Rosie, shower and water the garden. I was at the corner in good time and sat on the wall outside Georgios's taverna. It was not long before Bill came into view. Even at a distance I could see his hair was still wet from his shower; he was wearing jeans, a short sleeved shirt, trainers and carried a fleece over his arm. I watched and thought what a great guy he was and how over the past months he had become such a good friend. For the first time I allowed myself to look at him physically; not bad looking with his tousled blonde hair, tall and with a good physique for a guy in his late thirties. Yes, nobody would blame any woman for fancying him and I wondered why he had not had a string of dates over the season, either tourists or travel reps.

We ordered ouzo's at the kafenion and chose an outside table tucked away in the corner. Bill started the conversation by asking the questions; why had I decided to stay on and would I still be here when he returned next May? Good questions indeed. I felt I owed it to Bill to give him the full facts. We had plenty of time so I started from the beginning, a potted history of my life that culminated with my doctor's advice. As for my reason for not returning as planned, this was basically because I had enveloped myself in local life and I did not feel I had given myself enough time on my own, which was what the doctor prescribed and what Amy had been so horrified about when I originally told her about helping Despina at the shop. My original intention of solitude had gone out the window and I hoped by staying on through the autumn and winter months I would achieve this. As for being here next May; I had decided to return to the UK in early April. That was assuming I was able to hack a winter here and had not returned earlier. So no, I would not be here but hoped to visit sometime during summer months for a week.

All the while I talked, Bill listened intently and when I paused he asked Theo, who owned the kafenion, to fill our glasses; a total of three top ups by the time I had finished. I would have been light headed by then if it had not been for Theo, who brought us small plates of food; olives, beetroot salad, cheese and finally, small pieces of fried pork. When I had finished Bill leant across the table and took my hands in his.

"You sure have been through it Polly." he said looking sympathetically into my eyes.

"That's life." I told him. "Shit happens! What about you Bill, tell me about your life."

He looked a bit taken aback, swearing was something I tried to avoid but it slipped out and I put it down to the effect of the ouzos.

"I tell you what." he replied "Let's go over to the taverna and order some food and wine and I'll give you the low down over dinner."

This was the one and only taverna in Lionas that remained open throughout the year. It was run by Maria and Stelios who told us that during the season they produced a menu but now it was a case of going into the kitchen to see what was available and making our choice from there. We both chose the chicken pie which was made by Maria to the local recipe and with this we ordered the green beans in olive oil. We sat out in the lit courtyard; it was getting dark and the temperature was dropping so we were thankful of our fleeces to keep off the evening chill. Bill poured us a glass of wine each from our carafe of local house white, sat back in his chair and filled me in with his life's story.

"Very conventional start." he began, "Typical suburban background, parents who loved each other and me and my younger brother Matt. As I got older I failed to gel with the school regime, exams and all that. Particularly having to study subjects I had absolutely no interest in whatsoever. Upshot was I left as soon as I could and did odd jobs here and there during the winter and then it was the beach for me in the summer. Mum & dad were disappointed but knew it was pointless nagging me. I carried on like this for the rest of my teens and most of my twenties by which time Matt had secured a lucrative job in the air conditioning business, had married and provided my parents with two grandchildren, both girls. I had no plans to settle down and certainly not to marry; girls came easy in the summer, so why tie myself to one. Anyway, in my early thirties and with little interest in anything that did not involve either the beach or cars, I decided to get myself a regular job so I could buy a place of my own. I was at last beginning to grow up. I found I was good at selling cars and by saving the commissions for a few years, was able to put down a deposit on a small house within walking distance of the beach. It was shortly after I had got the place how I wanted it, sorted the garden and installed the all essential barbeque that I met Stella. She was so different to the other girls I had fleeting relationships with and we really hit it off from day one. We both had similar likes and the same life values and for the first time in my life; I fell in love. There wasn't anything I would not do for Stella. Life together seemed perfect, so I proposed and we married six months later. Thinking back, I have to say our wedding day was amazing. We married on the beach, Stella looked beautiful and my mum and dad were so proud. All went pretty well for the first year and then I began to get inklings that the twice weekly girl's nights out were nothing of the sort. It wasn't long after that Stella came home; announced she was pregnant and that it wasn't mine. I could have told her it wasn't mine; for the past three months she had done everything possible to avoid making love. She told me she was leaving and going to live with Ark, the baby's father. Despite having had my suspicions it still came as one hell of a shock and all sorts of things ran through my mind; mainly was I to blame for her going off with another man."

Bill paused while Maria brought our food to the table and asked if we needed anything else.

"Another carafe of wine would not go amiss." Bill told her before he continued.

"Well Polly to cut a long story short, Stella lost the baby, Ark threw her out and she had the confounded cheek to come back and ask for forgiveness. She told me she realised her mistake and thought we should have another go at our marriage. By then Polly, I had found out that Ark was not the first, so there was no way I was going to have her back. Instead I gave her a wad of notes out of my wallet and told to go and book into a hotel and also to get herself a lawyer. I wanted a divorce. So that is pretty well it. I divorced her, decided I needed a complete break and when I heard there was a job out here, I knew I could do no better. I closed the house up, left the keys with mum & dad, who are checking it every couple of weeks and booked a rather expensive flight here, via Athens. I have been well and truly burnt by that relationship Polly, one which started out so perfectly. When we first met Polly, and you said you would only entertain friendship and not a relationship, you have no idea what a relief that was for me. And then when you said, you were not that kind of girl and I got the wrong vibes and thought you were saying you were a lesbian; well what a start to a friendship! But it has been great hasn't it and just because I am going home does not mean it has to end here, does it?"

No it didn't. I told Bill I had planned to buy a laptop and once this was set up, hopefully with assistance from one of Yiannis's and Anna's sons, we could keep in touch easily over the winter months. The laptop would save me trips into town, although I felt if anything food shopping trips would become more frequent. By the time we had finished eating and had drunk all the wine, we were both a little light headed; in fact we were squiffy as we walked up the hill. Bill was happy to leave me at the junction with Georgios's taverna to walk along the dirt track. This was as long as I gave him three flashes with my torch when I reached my garden gate. This I did. It was not late, only about 10.30 p.m. but I was tired, not from physical exertion but from emotions of the day and the alcohol. I went straight to bed and was asleep as soon as my head touched the pillow.

We had just two days left before Bill's flight on Friday. Having exchanged potted life histories, we were now even more relaxed in each-others company. We spent Wednesday driving to the far end of the island where the colourful buildings of the small town of Agkonas were grouped round the fishing bay. We knew the bay attracted large expensive yachts in high season and we heard whispers of this or that celebrity who had been seen disembarking from their mega yacht. But in October the town had returned to day to day life providing a typical scene as you would see in any traditional fishing village. We chilled out and ate a substantial lunch of grilled fresh fish with salad and bread which we walked off afterwards by following a path that led up into the wooded hills. On Thursday, we left the car in Lionas, starting the day as we had on most Thursdays; with a walk and picnic breakfast at the ruined monastery. We continued on the paths and tracks that lead down to the beach, along the sands and then back up more paths and tracks. I had come to know all of these so well over the past few months. We stopped at the hamlet of Poulata but by then the one and only shop had closed for the afternoon. This meant lunch consisted of a couple of bananas left over from breakfast; these were rather bruised after bouncing all morning in my rucksack.

Panos had invited us both to join him and his family for dinner in the evening. Rather than leaving the Jimny outside the office in town, as previously arranged, we drove to their house on the outskirts of the main town. We had Bill's baggage with us for the return flight the following day. Bill was to stay overnight, I would return home by taxi and Panos would drive Bill to the airport in the morning. This, of course, meant that Bill and I would say our farewells on Thursday evening. I was happy with this arrangement as it would avoid any embarrassing emotional goodbyes on the Friday and I had promised Bill I would wave to his plane; assuming it took off in an easterly direction towards Lionas. It didn't quite work out that way.

Panos's house was impressive, he obviously did quite well out of the car rental business. He was there at the door to greet us and introduced us to his wife Ireni. The interior décor of the house was not to my taste. It had been designed by a friend of Ireni's and she was obviously very proud of their home with its mix of old and modern styling. Spiros and Maichail joined us for dinner which Ireni must have spent some considerable time preparing and cooking earlier that day. It was all delicious. In traditional Greek style we spent a long time at the table, passing the various dishes Ireni had cooked around several times. The meal complete, Spiros and Maichail cleared the table (this did surprise me) and then disappeared to their rooms.

"Lessons", said Ireni as they departed, which I took to mean homework.

Conversation flowed easily, with Panos occasionally translating for Ireni, and the evening passed quickly. I would have liked to have stayed longer but my taxi had been booked for eleven and all too soon we heard the driver sounding his horn. The two boys appeared immediately to say goodbye, Panos and Ireni both gave me a hug and told me if I needed anything during the winter months to let them know. Bill walked with me out onto the gravel drive, opened the door of the taxi put his arms round me and whispered in my ear

"'I am going to miss this island but most of all I'm gonna miss you Polly."

He then pulled back, kissed me on the cheek and as the tears started to form in my eyes, he pointed to interior of the taxi gesturing me to get in. Sat in the passenger's seat, with the window wound down, all I could manage was,

"Bye, miss you too." as the taxi started to roll down the drive.

Chapter 21

Back in Lionas, I was chastised by Rosie who was waiting on the veranda. I had left her plenty of food but she had been waiting for a few of her favourite treats before she went off for a nights hunting. She rubbed herself round my legs as I walked into the kitchen to the cupboard where I kept her food.

"Just you and me now." I told her. "It's going to be pretty quiet round here from now on."

I don't think she cared too much for company and she probably welcomed the lack of tourists walking back and forth along the track and vehicles kicking up dust.

I lay in bed feeling hollow and once again wondered if I had made the right decision to stay on. I repeatedly reminded myself that I could at any time go back to the UK and I would be going back anyway for Christmas. It was not until the early hours that I finally fell asleep and was woken at dawn by the sound of goat's bells as a herd passed further up the hill. Goat bells were a regular feature first thing and then again towards sunset but now there were little other noises, apart from birdsong, they sounded so much louder. I lay there thinking how perfect it would be if you could guarantee that the last thing you ever heard on this earth was the gentle ringing of these bells; so calm and peaceful.

Up and dressed I was not sure what to do; the days were getting cooler, particularly at each end of the day and soon I would have to put my shorts away. At the moment, provided I wore a fleece, it was still warm enough to eat breakfast on the veranda. I took out a tray with my cereal, a pot of yoghurt and a mug of tea and put this on the table and went back inside for some paper and pencil. I sat down and as I ate started to make a list for the day; weed the garden, water the garden, clean the bathroom, wash the towels, wave to Bill's plane etc. When I had finished eating, I screwed up the list, threw it down on the tray and pulled my phone out of my pocket. In a matter of minutes, it was arranged.

It was a favour; Thanassis was squeezing me in between other fares. He pulled up just after ten which left plenty of time. I had deliberately not changed and got into the passenger seat in my gardening gear; shorts, t-shirt, trainers and baseball cap. Thanassis looked at me quizzically,

"Airport?"

"Please" I replied.

"I think I understand." He continued, "You go to say goodbye to Bill. Very nice man." he winked "But like all summer people they go home. Some come back and some they don't."

And then there is me, I thought; the exception to the rule by staying behind.

It was quiet at the airport; just the one plane due to fly in and out again and that was Bill's flight to Athens. There would be plenty of taxis around when the flight landed but by the time the plane took off again it was more than likely the rank outside would be deserted. I arranged to phone Thanassis when I was ready to go back home and if he was busy he said he would make sure one of his friends picked me up. I paid him my fare and walked towards the departure door. The automatic doors opened onto the concourse where just one of the four desks was checking-in passengers. All the shutters on the shops were pulled down and locked with the exception of the café which remained open. Sat with his back to the doors and facing the departure board, which confirmed the flight was on time, was Bill, back hunched and as I got closer I could see his arms were resting on his knees. He was deep in thought and I tried to think of something witty to say as I put my hands on his shoulders. In reverse roles I am sure Bill would have come up with something but a simple,

"Penny for them." was all I could muster.

Surprised, he jumped up and turned towards me.

"Just thinking of you Polly and wondering if you were in your garden which by the looks of you – you have been!"

"Well, I thought you might like some company while you waited, so here I am."

He sat back down and I joined him.

"I have already been here an hour. Panos had some business to tend to so he dropped me off here first. I thought time would pass quickly but to be honest it has been an absolute drag. I started to think of what everyone would be doing in Lionas, going about their day to day business and how I was going to miss life on Aspros. I am really beginning to get depressed at the prospect of going home. I envy you Polly, staying on."

He looked so down in the mouth I tried to lighten his mood by reminding him he would be going back to warm summer weather in Australia whereas here, we were drifting towards winter and goodness knows what that was going to be like. We then went on to talk about the past months and the people we had met and although we shouldn't have, laughed about some of the visitors he had to deal with and the state some of the hire cars were returned in. When the concourse started to fill with passengers for the Athens flight we went outside and up onto the roof terrace to watch the plane land. It was not long before we could see it making its approach.

"Good job I came." I smiled "You'll be taking off in the opposite direction to Lionas. No way could I have waved to you."

We watched the landing and as the plane taxied towards the building the call requesting all passengers for the outgoing flight to go through controls came over the loudspeakers.

"Better go down, I hear the internal flight turn rounds are pretty quick." he said looking at his watch "Yes" he confirmed "Just half an hour to take-off."

So this was it, time for the final farewell.

"I won't come down if you don't mind. I'll stay up here and wave you off."

So we said all the silly things, like don't forget to email and hope to see you next year followed by a hug. Bill pushed me back, held both my hands, looked me up and down, smiled and said,

"Don't ever change Polly."

He picked up his rucksack and as the tears started to build uncontrollably in my eyes he turned and with no looking back he walked towards and down the stairs. Oh, how I hated farewells!

There were no seats on the roof terrace so I leant against the railings and watched the luggage being offloaded while a group of cleaners boarded the cabin for a quick tidy. A short flight, so there was no re-fueling and it seemed they had brought enough refreshments with them to cover both flights. The baggage carts were soon back on the tarmac loading cases and bags into the hold, the cleaners left the plane and shortly after, the first of the passengers made their way to the stairs. I watched intently for Bill but no sign until right at the end, there he was; the last passenger to board. He stood at the top of the stairs, waved, blew a kiss and then disappeared inside. I watched the plane taxi to the end of the runway where it waited for a few minutes before the pilot opened up the engines and the plane roared down the tarmac. There was no way of checking which side of the plane Bill was on or whether he could see me but I waved my arms all the same. The jet passed the roof terrace, the nose lifted and it climbed up into the skies, soon to be out of sight.

So that was it; Bill was on his way home and I was about to start living life here on Aspros in much the same way as the locals. I phoned Thanassis, he was having a coffee in town and would be at the airport in about twenty minutes. I made my way down from the terrace and sat near the taxi rank, which as predicted was empty. I began to postulate as to whether the friendship between Bill and I would carry on through exchange of emails or whether after the first one or two and when Bill was back into the swing of life in Australia, as to whether they would just fizzle out. Then there was the question of whether he would come back and work next May and whether I would be able to come back to the island for a holiday. Too many questions I told myself. Just have to wait and see. I did feel empty though and by the time Thanassis had dropped me off outside Stavros's and Despina's shop I began to consider taking that ferry on Sunday to Piraeus. Maybe it was not such a good idea to stay on.

Off course the shop was locked but I took the path round the side that led to the door of their adjoining house. The door was open into the kitchen and I could hear sounds of movement from inside so I called,

"Γεια, Πολέε του.", "Hello it's Polly."

"Ελα μέσα.", "Come in." I heard Despina reply.

She called to Stavros, who promptly appeared from further inside the house. He was grinning. Despina chastised him, saying there was nothing to smile about as their friend Polly was going home in a couple of days and that *she* was going to miss me even if he did not care.

"Ακούστε Πολέε." "Listen to Polly." Stavros said affectionately and nodded to me.

This was my cue, no point in waiting any longer,

"Θα μένω εδώ σε Λιώνας.", "I will be staying here in Lionas.", I smiled.

There was sheer delight on Despina's face.

"Ακριβώς για το χειμώνα.", "Just for the winter." I added but this did not discourage Despina's excitement.

It was Stavros who calmed her down by telling her to make us lunch while he found a bottle of wine. We sat out on their terrace at the back of the house which apart from a small block of studios had uninterrupted views across the sea towards the neighbouring island of Nithos. Despina brought out plates of courgette fritters, tomato salad, grilled peppers and keftedhes. Stavros opened the wine and the three of us sat in the early autumn sunshine. I couldn't have asked for a better start to my next five months on Aspros.

After I had helped Despina clear away the lunch things, I walked down to see Anna, stopping off briefly at home to check Rosie had all she needed. Anna too was delighted that I was staying and told me that I must tell Eva before anyone else did. I could not understand the urgency until Anna explained. Apparently when I arrived the local ladies viewed me with suspicion and were concerned I would turn out to be another Frieda. Frieda, she told me, was a young German woman who had come to the island in the late 1990's and like myself, planned to spend the summer here. She had immediately made herself unpopular by not associating with the local ladies; she refused their invitation to coffee in preference to sitting at the kafenion with the men folk. It went on from there,

"She flaunted herself." Anna said disapprovingly. "She never actually made a pass at the men but she would sit with her skirts pulled up and her knees apart while she fanned her face with a newspaper or whatever came to hand. She also thought she was the fountain of all Greek knowledge and would often be heard talking to visitors telling them about this and that and what you should and should not do. She actually knew quite a lot but it was the way she said it that riled everyone and there were times when she annoyed the visitors too. She had rented a small apartment with a roof terrace and it was this that proved to be her downfall." Anna paused, "You know we Greek ladies have a lot more control over our men than most people think. Yes, we may seem to be subservient but it is really us that control our families." she laughed, "We are quite skilful and can put things in our men's minds in a way they think an idea is their own. There is a lot of truth in the film My Big Fat Greek Wedding! What happened was Frieda took to sunbathing nude on her apartment's terrace. In fairness to her, I expect she thought nobody could see her but they did. It was a group of boys who saw her. They had made a summer camp in an old partially ruined house which has completely collapsed now. This was not far from the back of the apartments. A couple of the windows overlooked the terrace and this is where they got their viewpoint. Word soon spread and there was a steady stream of boys heading towards the house. Eva's friend, Elpida, spotted her grandson looking very suspicious as he walked up the alley to the ruined house. She followed him at a distance into the house and up the stairs where she caught about six lads tittering at the view. Elpida is a woman of some influence, a matriarch, and within hours the house was boarded up. Nobody really blamed or chastised the boys, after all they were just curious and being boys but from then on nobody would engage in conversation with Frieda. If she sat in the kafenion the men, as instructed by their womenfolk, moved their chairs away from her and although she was not barred from the shops, bars and tavernas, she did not receive a welcome. In under a week she was gone, the last person to see her was Georgios on his way to the taverna early one morning. She was pulling her case up through the village presumably to the bus stop. When I came here from the United States, village ways were very strange to me, as I am sure they are to you Polly. As you know topless sunbathing is frowned upon and nudity most certainly is not tolerated. This is the way it is in this part of Greece. I do sometimes wonder if she had not been German whether there would have been more tolerance towards her but there are a lot of islanders who still remember the horrors of the second world war and do not forgive easily. Anyway Polly, that is the reason why you were viewed with suspicion. In fact Stavros and Yiannis were given a bit of a rough time over you, firstly Yiannis for seeing if Stavros was willing to rent Maria's house and then Stavros for doing so. But Yiannis and I both gave our assurances that you had been an exemplary visitor in the past. Of course you passed the first test of coffee with the village ladies with flying colours and since then have proven that you respect and comply with local ways and traditions and look how you have helped us at the taverna, Panos in the car office and of course Despina too. You are liked and respected by us all. So Polly everyone will be delighted to hear you are staying for a few more months and you must go now and tell Eva so that she can spread the word, that is if Despina has not beaten her to it! She will be so pleased to know before Elpida. It will give her an edge in their circle of friends."

There were a few more things I wanted to talk to Anna about but they would have to wait. I heeded her advice and immediately set off up the hill to tell Eva. Walking back up, I no longer felt empty. Knowing that I was accepted had filled me with excitement of what the following months would bring. A quick look at my watch confirmed that, providing his flight was on time, Bill would have little time to wait now before he took off homeward bound. Eva's door was open; I knew I could walk straight in but English manners prevailed and I knocked on the door at the same time, calling her name. Eva always seemed to be busy, for a long term widow it amazed me what she found to do to fill her days. I heard her call from inside to come in. She was busy in the kitchen baking. A batch of tiropitas lay cooling on a rack while she was busy shaping biscuits ready for the oven. She looked up and smiled, pleased to see me. While the biscuits were cooking we sat in her living room with a glass of lemonade. Eva looked at me enquiringly; what was behind my unexpected visit? Usually when I popped in, I had something in particular to bring; vegetables from Stravros's allotment garden, some roses from my garden or because Eva did not have a phone, a message I had been asked to take to her. I took the plunge and told her in my best Greek I would be her neighbour for a few more months. She repeated what I said to make sure she had heard right and then got up from her straight backed chair and put her arms round me.

"Καλά, τόσο καλά. Δεν μπορώ να το πιστέψω, κάποιος κλείσει από τον χειμώνα.", "Good so good. I can't believe it, someone close by during the winter." she said and looked into my eyes. "Μακάρι να είχα μια κόρη, όπως και εσείς.", "I wish I had a daughter like you."

This took me aback, certainly not what I expected. When the biscuits were cooked I soon got the message that I should leave. Eva was dying to get the word around to her friends. She refused my offer to help clear away the bowls, baking trays etc. These would have to wait until later; Eva had more important things to do.

So that really should have concluded the diaries of my five and a half months on this small Greek island. The time I was to spend in the peace and quiet that only an island like Aspros can offer, time to reflect on my state of mind, to come to terms with my issues and to set myself on the right tracks so I could return to the UK and move forward positively.

Chapter 22

However, I decided to carry on with my diaries through into spring, which comes so much earlier in Greece than it does in the UK. I found sitting of an afternoon or evening logging my activities therapeutic. I carried on using notebooks although in some ways it would have been quicker on my laptop. One of the things I had wanted to talk to Anna about before she dispatched me up the hill to Eva's, was the purchase of a laptop. I knew her sons would be more computer conversant than I was. They would have more ideas when it came to choosing the right computer for my needs, setting up word processing in English and the all-important internet and email connections. I returned to Anna's on the Saturday afternoon to tell her Eva's surprising reaction and to ask if one of the boys would be in agreement to accompanying me into town some time.

"Could it wait until next Friday afternoon?" she asked. "Because if it can I can take you and Christos into the IT shop after school. I can bring the others back home and collect you later. Christos is the best at computers. When he gets time he is going to set up a website for the apartments and the taverna. But we two must go into town before then and get you an outfit for the wedding on Saturday."

"Wedding?" I enquired.

"Yes", replied Anna, "You remember when we bought my outfit. We went with Karis and Despina."

"Of course I remember but why do I need an outfit?"

"Because you will come with us as a guest, silly. Don't worry I will brief you on wedding etiquette. Weddings are so much fun, big family affairs with much laughter, dancing and of course, eating." she grinned

We decided on Monday morning for shopping. Anna would pick me up, drop the children off at school and we would continue into town.

Over the weekend I was filled with anxiety about my outfit. Would Anna expect me to wear something on the same lines and style as hers? I really would not be comfortable in anything figure hugging and definitely not in high heels or anything too bright. Maybe I had something in my wardrobe that would be suitable. No, everything was too casual for a wedding. I would have to stand my ground and not be talked into anything I was not happy with.

The first real rain for months fell on Sunday. It had a cooling effect and it also made the windows filthy, with the dust of summer sticking to the glass. I found a pair of socks to put on, changed my shorts for trousers and sat in the living room with my diaries. Rosie curled up next to me and apart from her occasional purring and the sound of the rain against the windows all was quiet. No pick-ups, hire cars or chatting tourists passing.

"This is how it's going to be from now on." I told Rosie who in response twitched her whiskers at the triviality of my comment.

The quiet of the afternoon was broken by the arrival of Stavros, there was a break in the rain and he had seized the opportunity to bring the heaters down for the house. Still in their boxes we unpackaged the oil filled radiators and put them around the house plugging in each one in turn. There was one for each of the bedrooms and the bathroom, two for the living room and a spare that I could either put in the hall or the kitchen. By the time we had finished there was a definite glow throughout and I watched Rosie stretch full length in appreciation. I offered to pay for the heaters. Stavros refused but said I would have to pay for the electricity, something up to now he had insisted was included in the rent.

After he had left, I turned the heaters off and put on the kettle.

"Time for a mug of tea." I told Rosie.

I had become much more appreciative of proper Greek coffee and their instant was certainly far more acceptable to those sold in the UK bearing the same brand names But there were times when there was nothing like a mug of tea and I was ever thankful to Amy for keeping me well supplied. As I sat down with my brew and one of Eva's homemade cinnamon biscuits I told Rosie we were going to be really snug in this little house.

On Monday I managed to convince Anna that the bright green dress and jacket she chose was not me and steered my way to a dress in the palest of blues. I felt comfortable in this and a pair of cream shoes and matching handbag finished my outfit off. I really did not want a hat or anything in my hair but at Anna's insistence I was persuaded to try some simple cream feathers mounted on a hair clip. I had to admit they did set everything off nicely. Pleased with my purchases, I treated Anna to coffee in the main square while she, as promised, filled me in on Greek wedding etiquette. Without the strains and pressures that came with high season, Anna was relaxed.

"We must come in for coffee on a regular basis" she commented, "and bring Despina with us and Karis too. Yiannis is keeping an eye on her this morning while he catches up on the accounts. We just don't have the time in the summer, apart from banking the takings and paying the suppliers but once he is up to date he will be out more. Not long now until he will be involved with the olive harvest. It's hard work but quite pleasurable all the same so if you fancy a bit of manual labour Polly come and join us. You don't have to stay all day, come back with me when I collect the boys from school."

I told Anna I would like to help, she just needed to let me know when and where. We had enough time to go to the internet café where I accessed my emails. Nothing much, just the usual update from Amy and one from Bill which I sent a brief reply to. He had a reasonably good trip back and was now looking for a job. My message was simple, just to say everything was fine here and that I would send him a longer update when I had my laptop, hopefully by this time next week.

Christos was as Anna had said; a whiz with computers. He took on board my requirements, decided which one on the shelves in the shop was most suitable for my needs, negotiated on the price and before long I had paid and Anna was back to collect us.

"If you leave it with me." he suggested, "I will set it up and then you can come to our house and I will show you the basics. As you don't have a phone line you will have to come down to us or somewhere else that has a modem so you can surf the net and receive your emails. All the other stuff you can do at home."

He looked at Anna and she nodded her approval that it would be okay for me to use their connection.

Christos worked quickly and I was able to collect my laptop on Sunday afternoon. After a brief rundown on the programmes, how to back-up, run scans and connect to other modems; I asked him if I could pay him for his time. I was not sure if this was the correct approach in the Greek way of doing things. He refused, smiled and said if I could help him with his English homework when he got stuck then that would be payment enough.

So there I was; set-up for the months ahead and if I were to cover these months in detail here in my book; well, it would be at least twice the length it is now so I will just settle for a few snippets.

I will start with social life. The thoughts I had of possibly being lonely and getting bored with my own company during the following months were soon dispelled. Firstly, there were the formal occasions such as the wedding as well as funerals and christenings all of which I was invited to and expected to attend. The wedding and christenings were joyous affairs with much laughter, socialising, music, eating and drinking. Funerals are quite different to those in the UK. For starters, there never seemed to be a long wait between death and internment (the Greek Orthodox faith frowns on cremations). Then there are the funeral processions, no great black hearses, but an open coffin followed by the mourners. The coffin lid was carried separately and as well as flowers, which would later lay on top of the grave, there were also what I can best describe as large lollypops of flowers. As for the service, there was no obligation to remain in the church throughout; it was quite common to see mourners leaving only to return later on in the service. But enough of death.

Name days, which are more important than birthdays, were another time for celebrations. These took place at a chapel, bearing the name of the person, and were usually built by the family. Many were up in the hills and most required a trip in a vehicle. In fact wherever their location there were vehicles involved to transport tables, chairs, food and crockery etc. Polly is a derivation of Mary the equivalent of which in Greece is Maria. This meant my name day fell on the same day as the Panagia, 15th August; the height of the season when only visiting Greeks had the time to celebrate. Later in the year November 21st was the name day for Despina and also unmarried Maria's. I suppose technically, with the divorce yet to be finalised, I was still married and maybe this only covered Maria's who had never been married at all but I took the opportunity to celebrate with Despina and joined in with the feverish preparations of food for what proved to be an exhausting but enjoyable day.

There were of course national and religious celebrations, such as Oxi Day in October. As I was spending Christmas in the UK and was returning home for good before Easter, I did not experience either of these major Ecclesiastical celebrations. I was however, there for Clean Monday on the 10th March, marking the beginning of the Orthodox equivalent of the period we, in the UK, more commonly refer to as Lent. Later in the month on the 25th March is Independence Day which marks the start of the war against the Ottoman Empire in 1821, when there were plenty of ceremonial parades, marching and flags to be seen in the town.

In the village it was customary to leave your house door open. Physically in summer but metaphorically in winter and it was to be expected for someone to just open the door and walk in for a chat during the colder months, or similarly I could do the same. This took a bit of getting used to as it was nothing to have three or four ladies of the village sat in my living room. Of course refreshments had to be provided which meant making sure there was always some fresh homemade biscuits in a tin. If the biscuits started to get stale, I either fed them to the chickens on the allotment gardens or to the passing goats plus, Stavros kept a bin where waste food could be left which he took periodically to his friend for the family's pigs.

Then there were visits to town, sometimes I went on my own on the bus for groceries, other times I would go with Anna, Despina and Karis to shop and have coffee or lunch, as well as the obligatory natter. Now the apartments were closed, Karis no longer spent time on a Thursday with Despina so she relished any opportunity to see Karis, who she had grown rather fond of.

Christos invited me to the school to meet his English teacher, who knew I had given him help and advice with his homework. After some coaxing I volunteered to help the students with their English orals. I spent one or two half-days a month with those students who struggled with the English language and those at the other end of the spectrum who had expressed an interest in moving away to an English speaking country. The latter benefited from picking up some of the idiosyncrasies and colloquialisms

146

that occur in any language. I enjoyed these sessions and there was always time for them to ask me questions about life in England. The most common questions were about our weather. Was it always cold, did it rain frequently and did it snow every winter?

Although it was cooler, there were days when the skies were crystal clear and the sun was warm enough at midday for me to sit outside on the veranda in a t-shirt. Walking was more enjoyable in the cooler months and I was able to cover greater distances without risk of overheating my feet and getting blisters. The beach was something else, devoid of sunbeds, towels and other tourist trappings, the bay was one gentle swathe of soft sand. I spent many an hour sat on the beach running the past through my mind and trying to come to terms with the problems of more recent years.

I had most definitely put the hysterectomy behind me. Children were not for me. I had come to the conclusion; I was not the maternal type. It wasn't a case of not liking children; otherwise I would not have agreed to help at the school. For me children came with commitments and responsibilities. Having no obligations suited me, plus there was a positive side to having no ovaries – no periods. This was a definite bonus with, no monthly stomach cramps, no making sure you always had tampons with you in case you came on early and no messed up underwear or leaks in the night!

As for Harry, well this would take a little longer. How could I have got it so wrong? How could I have fallen in love with him, made love with him, thrilled at his every touch and not realised or even had the slightest inkling that he was gay. Did I blame Harry? No, I don't know why but I didn't but I did blame myself and for a long time wondered what people thought about me and what they may be saying behind my back. I didn't imagine for one minute they exchanged sympathies for a marriage that

147

had seemed so perfect, where I had at last found someone who I loved and gelled with. But rather that they made a joke of it and laughed at my expense. Of course there was no proof I was victim of other's mirth but it felt that way and the thought niggled in my mind. It took some months before I could put all this behind me but what about Harry? I knew I would always have feelings for him but now more as a good friend, someone to talk freely and openly to and seek advice from. I was pleased he had found love and happiness with Mike and his emails had shown how they were excited about moving into a place of their own. Whether I would ever find anyone to love again in the true sense of the word remained a question unanswered.

Finally, there was Donald. I really thought I knew him but obviously not. What an inconsiderate piece of excrement he turned out to be! I had no idea of what his motives were for committing suicide; certainly nothing ever came out as a possible reason in the months following his death. How could he not leave a letter? Even though sympathy did not come easy from me, it must have been mind-shattering for Fiona to discover that in her thirties, he had made her a widow with two young children to raise and support. I never forgave him but spending time sitting on the beach in solitude mulling it all over helped me come some way towards pushing Donald further into the back of my mind.

Was I still on the verge of a nervous breakdown? Only a medical practitioner could tell me that but I was no longer having episodes of depression and being irrational or, periods of hopelessness, anger and irritability or, waking up in the night and not being able to get back to sleep because of all the things whirring round in my mind. Gradually these had become no longer an issue. All good signs and on a self-diagnosis basis I decided I was no longer 'on the verge' and had doubts as to whether I had actually ever been. The next thing was; how to move forward with my life. Going back to England for Christmas provided me with a number of aspects to consider.

Chapter 23

Amy went into labour early December. She phoned me while Alan was driving her to hospital and as a contraction started, she spluttered,

"Never again!"

After the contraction subsided she continued,

"Never again do I want to be as big as a bloody house. My boobs are like bloody udders and as tender as hell. The pain is excruciating. You'd think as it's my third it might just bloody well pop out."

She took a gasp and I heard her say,

"It's all your bloody fault, you are going to have to have the bloody chop Alan!"

I tried not to laugh, I heard women in labour can be abusive towards their baby's father but here I was hearing it first hand and as she was in the first stages; no doubt worse was to come. I told her to be calm, concentrate on her breathing and wished her luck.

"Luck", she retorted. "Need more than bloody luck. If It's anything like the other two, I won't be able to sit down for about a bloody week I'll be so bloody sore."

With that thankfully she hung-up. What had happened to calm Amy; 'bloody' had replaced her favourite word 'wow'. Poor Alan, did he really deserve this? It was five hours before the phone rang again; it was Alan.

"It's a boy." he announced triumphantly. "He's a whopping eight and a half pounds but I'll hand you over to Amy."

Before I could say 'congratulations' Amy was sobbing down the phone,

"Oh Polly, wow he's so beautiful, he has a wonderful mop of hair and I had forgotten how tiny fingers and toes could be. He's perfect, I can't wait for you to see him and I am so sorry. Alan told me I swore something awful earlier but I was in so much pain, I really did not know what I was doing or saying."

I laughed and told her I quite understood; which as I had never had a baby, I didn't. I told her to email me lots of photos and that it wouldn't be long before I was back for Christmas.

Indeed it was not long before I would be catching the ferry as I started my homeward journey. It would have been quicker to fly but flights back and forth to Athens were now only twice a week plus, airlines were in the habit of cancelling a flight if they had not sold enough tickets to make the flight economically viable. This could be a real problem for me with a connecting flight booked onwards to Heathrow If there were storms, ferries were likely to be delayed but Yiannis advised me that of the two, the ferries were more reliable.

The days were getting colder; necessitating the purchase of a couple of quite expensive jumpers in town. I resolved to find time to buy some thick tops in the post-Christmas sales and sort through and select some warmer clothes which had been packed away in the flat. There was little to arrange before I left, apart from asking Eva to look after Rosie in my absence, which she agreed to willingly. Stavros said he would check the house over every few days to make sure all was okay. I was all set to go on the morning of the 20th, with some presents in my rollbag along with a couple of changes of clothing, my make-up and jewellery and a few favourite toiletries. I took my laptop as hand luggage along with a couple of books to keep me occupied during the journey. The books were picked out earlier in the year from the 'library' Anna kept for visitors at their studios. Yiannis drove me to the port of Gemara in his old red van. He smiled his cheeky grin as I thanked him and we exchanged farewells. He drove off into the town bibbing his horn and waving out of the window. There was plenty of time, before boarding the ferry, to have a coffee in a small café opposite the quay and to check both my passport and tickets were easily to hand.

Once foot passengers started boarding, I did likewise and found a seat inside mid-ship. If it was choppy there would be less dipping and rolling in this position; well that was the theory anyway. We stopped at several islands before finally docking at Piraeus late afternoon. I had a room booked for the night at a nearby hotel which was just a three minute walk to the stop for buses linking to the airport. Yiannis had told me to stay close to the hotel. Taking his advice, I found the restaurant he recommended easily; it was just a couple of streets across from the hotel. Specialising in grills, I enjoyed a plate of mixed meats, a salad, bread and a couple of glasses of wine for what I considered to be a very reasonable price, given its location. After breakfast the following morning I took the bus to Athens Airport and checked in for the midmorning flight to Heathrow. With the difference in time, the whole journey took me a little over twenty four hours, although with all the sitting on the ferry, bus and plane, it felt longer!

Diane was there to meet me and after hugs, a coffee and a brief catch-up, we walked to the car park where, as arranged, my car had been brought ready for me to head off to the hotel I had booked for a couple of days. Diane was visibly anxious to get back to the office, always a busy time before Christmas with clients wanting last minute shipments processing, so she went on her way while I got into my VW Golf thinking how strange it felt to be behind the wheel after so many months away. Even stranger was getting to grips with the volume of traffic; it had not taken long for me to forget how congested this area could be. Before flying out to Aspros, I got a buzz out of moving from lane to lane on the M4 and zipping round the roundabouts but now it gave me no pleasure whatsoever. In fact it was scary.

I checked into the hotel on the outskirts of Slough. Despite the tree and decorations in the reception area, it felt very impersonal but the room was spotlessly clean, functional, a good size and it had a TV; something I had managed without on Aspros and to be quite honest, hadn't missed either. Double glazing protected me from the noise of the incessant movement of traffic on the A4 and the thermostat for the central heating provided me with almost as much warmth as a summer's day on Aspros. Harry and Mike were going to Scotland for Christmas and the New Year; Mike had never been north of the border and was keen to photograph the snow-capped mountains and the festivities over Hogmanay. While they were away, I had the use of the flat and when they returned I would go back to the hotel for a few days before flying to Athens on the 5th January. This way I did not put anyone out over the holiday period and more importantly; I could do what I wanted when I wanted rather than taking up the hospitality offered by Amy's parents and having to fall in with their regime.

My first port of call on the following morning was to see Amy. She was right, baby Thomas was a stunner with a mop of dark hair and huge eyes. It was impossible not to smile adoringly at his beauty. There was a lot to cram in before I returned, including meetings, at the office, with my bank manager, solicitor and accountant. Then there was the flat to sort. This involved retrieving all my clothes and personal items and putting on one side some warm sweaters and trousers to take back. The remainder were boxed and transferred to a warehouse lock-up I had arranged to rent. I often wondered why these lock-ups were so popular; apart from company's storing their old paperwork rather than paying premium office space rates. After depositing my boxes, I asked the question. Virtually anything and everything was the response, from toys children had outgrown, excess furniture after a property move or during a property extension. The list went on with me falling into the working abroad category, only technically I had not been working but helping out.

I also fitted in a visit to my doctor and dentist. I had already contacted my doctor, after deciding to stay on Aspros over the winter, to arrange my repeat prescriptions. She made it quite clear that she wanted to see me when I came back in December. She seemed a little taken aback when I walked into the surgery and commented on how good I looked and how she felt I was more relaxed. She likened me, before I went away, to being like a coiled spring; one she was not sure which direction it would release itself. Hence her diagnosis of 'being on the verge of a nervous breakdown'. She wanted to know what I had been doing, frowned when I told her about helping Despina and at the taverna and car hire office but nodded in approval at my more recent periods spent in reflection on the beach. I came away with a virtual clean bill of health and instructions to carry on as I had been and to come back and see her on my return in the spring.

It wasn't only my doctor who remarked as to how much more relaxed I looked. Everybody did and with all the social events over Christmas, meeting up with most of my friends and the office staff; it was all very encouraging.

Christmas Day proved busy but fun. I drove to Amy's and Alan's after breakfast to help with preparations for lunch. Despite both Amy's and Alan's parents offering to have Christmas at theirs they insisted on spending it at home so baby Thomas could maintain his routine. Plus the children would not have the problem of deciding which of their new toys to take with them before everyone bundled into the car and driving to whichever of the grandparents were to be graced with their presence. With both sets of grandparents coming for the day, it was quite a houseful and fortunately for Amy, Alan's mum, Jane, had taken on the task of shopping for the food while Amy's mum, Ruth, had made the pudding and cake and the two dad's Ron (Alan's dad) and John (Amy's dad) had between them sorted the drinks both alcoholic and soft. With everything under control food and drink wise, this left me with the problem of what I could provide. With little time for shopping, I settled for some rather extravagant crackers, spotted in a department store in Windsor, branded as being suitable for families of varying ages, plus a florist near the flat was able to produce a last minute festive arrangement for the table.

Jane and I took over the kitchen, we worked well together, while the others took turns to play with the children and keep everyone plied with drinks. As Amy was breastfeeding and I was driving, we kept each other company sampling the range of soft drinks. It was a wonderful family day and I felt privileged to be included. After tea when Jane and I had finished the washing up, I made my excuses; I wanted to email friends in Aspros. I left them to put the children to bed and to play board games. Back at the flat, there was a bottle of wine waiting for me in the fridge, not just any wine but a bottle produced in a vineyard on Aspros using the indigenous Greek grape, Assyrtiko. I brought the bottle back with me and sipping this fruity aromatic wine while I answered emails, was the perfect way to round off the day. It was 9 o'clock before I had finished and sat back on the sofa. While feeling mellow from the half bottle of wine I had consumed, I received a text. It was Bill, 'Where are you? Is it OK to phone?' I didn't reply but called his number straight away. I knew it would be expensive but what the heck! I wasn't sure exactly what the time was out in Australia but it turned out is was seven, Boxing Day morning. It was great to talk to him. Although we had exchanged regular emails since Bill went back, we hadn't actually spoken since he left Aspros. It wasn't until we started chatting that I realised how much I had missed his company over the past few months and by the time we hung up I could feel tears gently pricking at the back of my eyes. As the tears started to roll down my face, I told myself not to be so stupid, poured another glass of wine and turned on the TV. I was pretty squiffy by the time I went to bed. This was not a problem as I had nothing arranged for Boxing Day until the evening when Diane had invited me round for dinner.

With no idea as to exactly what I was letting myself in for, I volunteered to babysit for Amy and Alan on New Year's Eve. They had been invited to a dinner party at a friend's house and as their usual sitters were all out partying I stepped into the breach. Both Emily and Daniel were ready for bed when I arrived and Thomas was sound asleep in his crib. Both the children were very good and after they had finished watching Chitty Chitty Bang Bang they meekly went upstairs, used the loo, washed their hands, cleaned their teeth and settled in their respective beds for me to read them a story. Soon asleep, I turned out the light and pulled their bedroom door to; leaving a gap so the light on the landing provided a slight glow in their room. It was ten when Thomas woke up for his bottle of Amy's expressed milk. I was really apprehensive about the whole feeding, burping and changing thing but managed. Getting him back down again was another thing. Every time I put him in his crib he screamed and when I picked him up, so he did not wake Emily and Daniel, he stopped. After about four attempts, I gave up and took him back downstairs with me. Cradling him in my arms I watched some pretty dire programmes on the TV. I must have fallen asleep and missed seeing in the New Year because it was the sound of Alan's car pulling up on the drive at about 1 a.m. that woke me. Thomas was fast asleep, so I quickly but gently took him upstairs and put him in his crib and was just coming back down when Amy walked through the front door.

"Everything okay?" she asked apprehensively.

"Fine" I replied and told her I had just put Thomas back in his crib.

When Alan came in, after putting his car in the garage, we exchanged hugs and kisses and best wishes for a

Happy New Year and then I left them to have some quiet time to themselves before Thomas woke for his 2 a.m. feed.

Festivities over, Harry and Mike returned on the afternoon of 2nd January. Mike was full of Scotland and insisted I did not leave the flat immediately so he could show me some of his photographs. I had not realised they would be sporting kilts for the Hogmanay celebrations until they showed me a photo another guest had taken of the two of them. It was plain to see how relaxed they were in each other's company and how much in love they were. I told them I had already moved my boxes into storage and was pretty sure there was nothing of mine left in flat but if they did find anything to either bin it or take it to a charity shop. Before I left to spend the last three nights of my stay in the impersonal hotel in Slough, we had a quick discussion about the progress of the sale of the flat.

The next two days were spent tidying up odds and ends, spending time with Amy and in the office. I sensed an atmosphere in the office, nothing to do with the business, more to do with my lengthened stay on Aspros. Yes, there was a definite feeling of resentment and perhaps one of me being selfish by leaving them to get on with things rather than facing my responsibilities. Quite understandable really but not enough to make me have second thoughts and stay.

Amy took me to the airport in my Golf which I left for her to use as she wished. Her car was getting old and unreliable and it pleased me to know she could use my car until I returned, when hopefully they would have found a replacement for her cranky and clunky Fiesta. Amy was tearful to see me go but I was excited. I could not wait to get back to Aspros, to my little house and Rosie. I was surprised how much I had missed Rosie; there were times at the flat when I found myself talking to her!

Chapter 24

I took the evening ferry out of Piraeus and settled in my cabin before sampling some of the dishes available in the restaurant and relaxing with a glass of wine. Of course, if I was going to get any sleep, it would take more than just the one glass. Three glasses of wine and one of ouzo later and thankful that so far the crossing had been smooth, I made my way back to the cabin. Despite the intake of alcohol, sleep did not come easy. Firstly there was the throbbing of the engines and then there was the excitement of seeing everyone again. Even though I had only been away for two weeks, it seemed like an age. I also felt a little apprehension. The weather in December had been cold, the winds brisk and the periods of rainfall far heavier than I had imagined. Would I be able to cope over the next couple of months? Stowed in my bag in the cabin was my warm clothing from the flat plus, new jumpers, a waterproof jacket and a pair of wellies. All I could do was wait and see.

When I caught the morning bus from the top road which runs from the port of Gemara to the main town, I often wondered why some of the passengers looked so exhausted. After a restless night on the ferry, I now knew why. I had planned to catch the bus from the port but Anna was there to meet me. She had no idea what a welcome sight she was. After hugs and kisses, Anna looked at my bulging bag quizzically.

"Christmas presents?" she asked.

"Some", I replied, "As well as jumpers and socks and other things to keep me warm."

Anna just laughed. As already said, I had only been away two weeks but as Anna drove back to Lionas, I took in the vistas as though I had been away for two years. It was wonderful to be back and there waiting for me on the veranda was Rosie. She meowed loudly when I got out of the 4x4. I swear she was telling me off! Anna had turned on the heaters and left some milk, bread, butter and wine in the fridge. There was also a couple of tiropitas, a dish of stifado and some vegetables which Eva had brought to the house the previous day.

"Should be enough to get you through today." Anna pointed to the shelves as she opened the fridge door. "I am going into town tomorrow, so if you would like to come with me and stock up your cupboards, be at the end of the road just before eight when I come past with kids."

I nodded and gave Anna another hug.

"Right", she said "I'm off to tackle a pile of ironing and take over from Yiannis who has been keeping an eye on Karis. If you get bored; I've got a spare iron." she laughed and walked down the path to the car.

A quick bib on the horn and she was gone.

I left my bag on the floor in the lounge and sat down on the wooden settle. Rosie jumped up and as she curled herself round on my lap she started purring. I had a strange feeling, almost a numbness that I couldn't explain. A bit like when you get back from holiday and try to think of all the things you need to do to catch up and don't know where to start first. But then on the other hand, it was nothing like that at all. I stroked Rosie for about half an hour and then remembered my bag. I gently lifted her to a chair, unzipped the bag, had a quick rummage and pulled out a sealed bag.

"Look, Rosie." I said shaking the bag. "I brought these back for you, genuine English cat treats. What do you think?"

Judging by the increased purring as she crunched the small cat biscuits – scrumptious!

I was soon back in some kind of day to day routine but the weather which, as I have mentioned had turned decidedly colder at the beginning of December was now much colder than I anticipated. It wasn't just the cold but the damp and the winds too. There were times when I wondered whether I should pack my bag rather than continue suffering the conditions. The heaters were on all day, taking the chill off the house but it was no good sitting huddled round them trying to keep warm. It was far better, provided it was not raining torrents, to take a brisk walk down to the beach and back. Not only did this get the blood pumping but I also appreciated the warmth in the house on my return. If it was raining hard then there was no alternative but to stay indoors. Jogging on the spot to warm myself, Rosie peered at me in disdain, as if to say 'Why don't you curl up in a ball like me.' The rain brought the damp which left the walls moist and because they did not get the opportunity to dry properly, mould grew. The only answer to the mould problem was periodically cleaning the offending areas with a bleach solution. This removed the unsightly black but it was not long before it was back again. Overlooking the sea provided magnificent 'to die for' views in summer but in winter the winds blew across the water, straight up, hitting the front of the house making the shutters rattle and the gate swing on its hinges. Luckily the back of the house was afforded some shelter but there were nights when I was woken by the howling, buffeting gusts which reached such force I thought the roof may blow off. I had to brace myself to take a shower, even though most days there was warm water from the tank on the roof, the temperature was a long way short of the power shower we had in the flat back in the UK. I left my towel on one of the heaters, with my underwear covered with my top clothes on another in the hall. This way I had something warm to dry myself with and warm clothes to put on afterwards. I used all the blankets, stored in the cupboard at the end of the hall, on my bed and made sure I had a hot drink before I retired. Rosie, who now spent more time inside, curled up next to me on the bed, keeping me awake with her purring. Heating the house proved to be expensive, electricity prices were high on the island, but I had to have the radiators on and just bite the bullet and paid out when the bills came. But it wasn't like this all the time.

There were days when it was bright and I walked down to the village and sat with a coffee under the plane tree before buying my day to day necessities from the shop. Most weeks I went into town with Anna and Despina for lunch and a chat. I regularly visited Eva for a lesson in Greek and when I had taken in as much as I could in a session, she related stories about villagers and the surrounding countryside in simple language that I could understand. If I could not comprehend she would rephrase so I could. I learnt a lot from Eva.

By February there was a distinct feel that spring was round the corner. With the warmer days, life was starting afresh. It felt good.

Chapter 25

By the end of February, my mind was made up. I would not return to the UK in April, I had no inclination to resume my life as it had been. 'Why should I?' I asked myself on several occasions. There is more to life than working flat out to afford a home (the flat was more like an apartment with three bedrooms, two bathrooms, lounge with a balcony, dining room, kitchen and study) fitted out with all the modern appliances and quality furniture, a top of the range car, stylish clothes and expensive wining and dining. No, I had left this all behind; this lifestyle was my past. I would live here on Aspros, where I would be prudent, economical and most important - Happy.

And so in a way that brings my diaries to an end. Covering my life from hereon in any detail would entail another book! However, I will carry on for a little longer with my continuing life on Aspros and how things are for me today. To keep this as concise as possible, I have put this under headings, starting with:-

Finances
I was determined to be self-sufficient as far as was practical and only dip into the money from the sale of the flat and my half of the business, to fund rent and winter electricity. Selling the business was not straight forward and best described as a messy affair. It did not pan out the way I wanted it to but it was obvious things could not carry on with me as a director and 50% share owner.

Funding my lifestyle was achieved, as many Greeks do, with multiple employments. Yiannis liked the way I met and greeted customers at the Blue Sea and took me on as an employee for four evenings a week. The school paid me for one half day a week to continue to help students with their English orals. Despina and Stavros insisted on paying me to help in the shop while Stavros was out on caretaker duties. I obtained the necessary insurance cover and took out groups of walkers at each end of the season for rambles in the locality. With my local knowledge and stories Eva had told me, as well as my own understanding of the indigenous flora and fauna, I was able to add extra interest to these walks. Taking on one of the smaller allotments I grew fruits and vegetables which provided a seasonal income. The local tavernas and supermarket bought most of my produce and the rest I either ate or sold from the house. A small flock of chickens took up a large portion of the back garden. I had no problem selling the eggs particularly to the tourists, who raved about their freshness and deep orange yolks. And if they needed help at the Hermes office, I took a payment for this. Multiple employment incomes made my end of year tax returns, taxing to say the least!

Amy

I am sure Amy will agree with me, when she reads my account of life on Aspros; we have gradually grown apart. It was bound to happen with us both living so far away from each other and both leading such different lives. Life in Berkshire is so very different from that on the small Greek island of Aspros. For a few years Amy and Alan brought the children here for holidays. I looked forward to their annual visit, when the schools broke up in July, but as Emily and Daniel got older it was clear Aspros no longer provided the amusement their peers at school experienced on their holidays. It was time for the family to find another destination. We still exchange emails and photo's on a regular basis, we Skype and I send the children presents for birthdays and Christmas. I can never thank Amy enough for her support and just being there when I was going through my difficult period and was 'on the verge'. Amy has given me far more than I have ever been able to give her in return.

Harry and Mike

Following the sale of the flat and the divorce, I decided to keep out of their lives. We exchange Christmas and birthday cards and the occasional email. They now live in a mews house in Windsor and enjoy an active social life, eating out and entertaining friends. Living in such a historic town they are never short of visitors who come to see the castle, the adjacent network of back lanes with curio shops and to sit by the River Thames.

Yiannis, Anna and their Family

All provided me with support in one way or another over the years. Anna is a good friend who I can always turn to. Dimitri went off to do National Service. When he went, he was a rebel; on his return, he was a man. Karis adored her elder brothers, as they did her and she has retained a strong affection for Despina.

Despina & Stavros

Each year I tried to negotiate an increase in the rent I paid for the house. Each year Stavros would hear none of it. However, he did let me pay for the paint when it needed sprucing up. We had an arrangement that I decorated the interior and he painted the exterior. While he painted, I weeded his allotment or helped in the shop. Like Anna; Despina has been a good friend and when the tourists went home we spent many a morning chatting and making jewellery ready for the next season. Initially making jewellery was an experiment. Whilst surfing the net, I found you could buy online, beads, threads, clasps and all manner of items used to make jewellery. I suggested we buy a selection, which we did, used our creativity, although mine is a bit limited, and produced earrings, necklaces and bracelets to sell the following year. Branded as 'Handmade in Aspros'; they sold like hotcakes. The following year we expanded and increased the range. They continued to be popular and as the jewellery was so much cheaper to produce than buying in ready-made items; the shops profits increased.

Maybe this was the reason why Stavros would not let me pay any more in rent.

Jane Wilkins

Although I never received any further communications from Jane Wilkins, a couple of years ago I had one of those 'I've seen you somewhere before.' moments. I was doing my meet and greet bit at the Blue Sea, which included taking orders for both drinks and food. Apparently, I was very good at explaining some of the more unusual dishes on the menu, promoting the dishes of the day as well as reciting ingredients to those who had food allergies or special dietary requirements. Anyway, one particular evening in July two couples walked in and as I showed them to a table I was aware one of the women was looking at me intently. It was then that I had this 'I've seen you ....' moment. It was while I was bringing their drinks to the table that I remembered where. It was on the family photo that Jane Wilkins had sent me. She was my half-sister. I felt a wave of panic come over me and moved away from the table swiftly. The only way to tackle the situation was to carry on as normal. I did. Although, during the course of the evening, I was aware of her watching me, I made no eye contact. When they left she said,

"Goodnight Polly."

Did she really recognise me or had someone called my name during the evening? I really could not tell. I can only assume that if she did recognise me she wanted no more to do with me than I did with Jane Wilkins or her family. At home, I dug out the photo from the storage box under my bed, yes, there she was. Jane Wilkins had written the names on the reverse. It was Claire. I did not see her again.

Eva

Dear, dear Eva. Over the years we have become closer and I have come to love her. I believe Eva is the nearest I will ever get to having a mother. Not only did she help me to speak the Greek language but she showed me how to cook her way. Some of her dishes were simple, others complicated but all used only the freshest local ingredients. If I did not follow her instructions, she would gently smack me on the back of the hand and we would both laugh. She took me out into the countryside, showing me the best places to find horta (Greek greens) and after it had rained we collected snails. Eva showed me how to clean them before cooking, how to cook them with potatoes, courgettes, onions, garlic and dill and then how to eat them. How she chastised me the first time when I turned up my nose as I put the first snail into my mouth and then when I tasted how good they were and smiled in appreciation, she simply said,

"Δείτε!" "See!"

Eva was full of tips, ideas and recommendations on how to do this or that. I owe her so much.

Rosie

There was something special about Rosie. What drew her to come and live with me, apart from a reliable source of food, I don't know. I never knew how old she was or whether she had a previous owner. Because she was so friendly from day one, I don't believe she was feral. Although she spent a good amount of time in the warmer months out hunting or curled up in a shady place in the garden, in winter she proved to be a great companion, spending most of her time indoors either curled up near a heater or on my lap and during the night, on my bed. I never understood why she did not bring other cats back; in fact she was quite positively hostile to any feline that dared to trespass on her territory. That was until one day in late August when she walked in the door with a young tabby cat in tow. She made me laugh as she gave the youngster what seemed to be a guided tour of the house, finishing in the kitchen where there was always a bowl of dried cat food and another of water on the floor. From then on the tabby was a regular, sometimes coming in with Rosie or boldly walking in on its own. It soon allowed me to pick it up; this was when I discovered it was a tom and I knew I would have to keep my eye on him in case, when he reached cat puberty, he started squirting the furniture. After a couple of weeks I decided it was time the youngster had a name. I called him Ari because he walked as proud as a lion. He took to his name and responded to it well. As Ari flourished, I could see Rosie was deteriorating. She became slower, spent more time sleeping and ate less. By the mid-October I was seriously contemplating taking her to the vet in town but before I had made an appointment, she died. I had been out early in the morning to tend my allotment and when I left Rosie came outside with me, to lay in the garden in the autumn sunshine. I knew the warmth would do her good but on my return, she lay motionless on the veranda. I don't believe I have ever cried so much. I left her until rigor mortis set in before burying her (I did not want to make any mistakes) in the garden. Ari was with me as I shovelled the soil over her body and it was then that I realised why she had brought him back to live with us. She knew her demise was imminent and she had found me a new friend, Ari, to take her place.

Bill

In some ways Bill took the place of Amy as my best friend but he became more than that. As soon as I had decided, at the end of February, to stay on Aspros I phoned Bill. He was over the moon I would be here when he returned in late April and when he did, we took up from where we left off. I really had missed him and found it impossible to hide my tears when he flew back to Australia in the October. By the following year we had both got over our previous marriages and were ready for new partners; we became a couple. As to how and when we did is between us two, so no tales of making love in the olive groves or rolling naked in the sands! Which by the way we didn't! Suffice to say writing this has filled the veins in my cheeks. Whenever he walks in the room I feel a surge within me, the kind of feeling that any woman who has loved and wanted a man will understand. Bill wanted to stay throughout the year but finances dictated his return to Australia each autumn. For us the saying 'absence makes the heart grow fonder' was true and each April I would be almost jumping with joy as he walked through arrivals at the airport. Not the ideal way for a couple to live but it worked and after all, military personnel are often posted away from home and families for lengths of time so it was by no means a unique relationship. I asked Stavros's permission for Bill to come and live with me.

"Of course, of course, I wish you both much happiness." was his response.

Friends in Aspros were delighted for us and there was no tutting or scowling from older members of the community because we were not married.   The arrangement worked well until Greece's economy went into recession in 2008. At first there was little change but by 2010 cut backs were starting to take their toll and for Bill it meant there would not be a job for him in 2011. Panos's eldest son had been unable to secure employment after finishing college and so the only available employment was in the family business; running the office in Lionas. Bill told me how upset Panos was when he told him but at times like this, family has to come first.   Bill too was upset but also understood.   The toughest part was; Bill could not afford to come back unless he had employment.

Chapter 26

That day in July when Panos broke the news; we sat outside on the veranda in the evening both feeling devastated. Passers-by on their way back to the Golden Sun bungalows must have wondered why, in such a beautiful location, we looked so glum. As the sun began to set, Bill took my hands in his and looked me in the eyes.

"This does not have to be the end. The setting sun marks the end of the day, tomorrow when it rises there will be a new day and a fresh beginning. It can be the same for us; tomorrow can be a fresh beginning for us too."

Looking at him quizzically, I asked.

"What do you mean?"

"I want you to come back with me in October. I want you to come and experience life in Australia and if you don't like it we will find another country to live in that you do like. Polly, I don't want to be without you. I love you too much to be without you." He paused before continuing, "Don't give me an answer straight away, think about it. But now I think we need to eat. Come on, we'll walk to Georgios, he will cheer us up."

And cheer us up he did. Georgios was particularly jovial, probably because the taverna was pretty well full. Whether he sensed our mood I am not sure but after seating us at a table he whispered,

"Tonight, we forget the menu. I have something very special that I want to share with you both. But first ouzos!"

We got chatting with a couple on the adjacent table who I had seen when I was working at the Blue Sea and who had been to see Bill to book a car. They introduced themselves as Grace and Mark and like so many other tourists they wanted to know if we lived on the island. Between us we explained what we did which, apart from Bill returning to Australia each October, they thought sounded the perfect lifestyle. They were really intrigued

169

with the walks I led and as they seemed such a nice genuine couple and although I normally stop leading walks at the beginning of July, I agreed to take them on a short walk the following morning.

Georgios's 'something very special' was a goat dish which he served us along with dishes of potatoes cooked in the oven, green beans in olive oil and a basket of bread.

"I don't put this on the menu." he explained quietly as he bent his head over the table, "because some people are, what you say, 'squeamish' about eating goat, in the same way they are about rabbit, so I stick with chicken, pig, cow and sheep. But this has been cooked this afternoon in my kitchens for my friends and staff."

It was all delicious and as there was so much meat and as Grace and Mark seemed more adventurous than the run of the mill tourist; when Georgios was busy at the till we gave them some chunks of goat to try. They were as equally impressed as we were with the succulence and flavour of the goat meat. When we had finished eating, we invited them to join our table where we all drank a little too much wine before rounding the evening off with Greek coffees and Metaxa brandies.

In theory, after all that alcohol, I should have slept like a baby but that night while Bill snored softly, I lay awake for several hours until in the small hours I fell into an exhausted sleep. While I lay awake, I mulled over Bill's offer and tried to weigh up the pros and cons but my mind was too fuddled with alcohol to think straight and make a rational decision. This would have to wait until the next day.

Grace and Mark arrived just after 9.30 a.m. and we set off along the path towards the ruined monastery. It was already hot and the sky was a radiant blue as we walked slowly, making frequent stops in the shade to refresh ourselves with sips of water. As our progress was slow, I was able to impart pretty well all of the local history I had learnt over the past years; in particular the devastation caused by the earthquake almost sixty years ago. I told them about the occasional tremors that occurred from time to time and how frightening it was the first time I felt the house and all its contents shaking. Now, I took the tremors in my stride but if they occurred when I was indoors; I made a quick exit – just in case! It was a relaxing morning, returning to my house just after midday. If I had a particularly pleasant group of walkers, I invited them back to my garden and gave them glasses of my homemade lemonade and biscuits. The only problem with this was, getting them to leave! On our return, I asked Grace and Mark to join me for some light refreshments which they gladly accepted. They sat on the veranda while I prepared a simple selection of dishes; diced cheese, olives, beetroot with garlic in olive oil and sliced tomatoes with oregano. I took these out on a tray along with plates and glasses and from the fridge, a bottle of chilled white wine. I brought out a chair from inside and we spent a pleasant hour chatting, with Grace looking round the garden and at my invitation, they both had a brief look round the house.

"This is just perfect." Grace gasped, "We would love to rent a village house like this for our holidays. When we looked on the internet and through the brochures the only places we could find for rent were either large expensive villas or small purpose built studios or apartments. But if we could rent a house like this, I don't think I would want to go home. It's just perfect." she repeated.

Yes, Grace was right; just perfect.

They did not outstay their welcome and as they left, Mark tried to push a ten euro note into my hand. I refused point blank, telling them I had enjoyed their company and they had paid for the brandies yesterday evening so we were all even.

"Do you mind if I take a photo of your house?" Grace asked.

"No of course not. I'll shut the door and step off the veranda."

"Well, if it's not too much of a cheek, would you mind being in the photo too?"

"That's OK. So long as you don't stick me on Facebook or anything like that." I laughed.

Such a nice couple I though as they walked off along the track. So close, they're meant to be together.

Bill closed the office during the afternoons and was usually back just after two for lunch and during the hotter months; this was followed with a siesta. If I was to have time to myself to make a decision or at least try to, I needed to be gone before he returned. I left a note with the various options for lunch, said I had gone to the allotment to root water and would tell him about this morning's walk later. I put water, bread and cheese for lunch in my rucksack along with my notebook and a pen.

I did a little root watering, taking care not to splash the foliage. If I did, the sun would undoubtedly scorch the leaves. Sitting down in the shade of a large mulberry tree, I ate my bread and cheese and drank copious amounts of the water before pulling out my notebook and pen. The pros and cons had been whizzing round my head and if I was to make a rational decision I needed to write all of these down. I started a list on the left side of the page with the positive and negative points of staying on Aspros and on the right side I did the same for Australia. The plus points for Aspros far outnumbered those for Australia. Unlike Bill I could support myself almost indefinitely on Aspros. If, due to the cutbacks, I lost most or all of my jobs I would still be able to take the walks and I could apply to be a travel rep. I could also use the money from the flat and business, which I referred to as my savings. Lists completed, I had a short doze before reading through the pros and cons once again. Yes, all the points were covered but I had not come to a decision. Despite Aspros having a definite lead over Australia, it was not as simple as that. There was one particular positive, which was carrying more weight than any of the others but even so my mind kept wavering back and forth. No point sitting there any longer, I gathered everything up, walked slowly back home and sat on the veranda until Bill woke from his siesta. While I waited I listened to my MP3 player. My mind was in such a buzz and at times like these I found music provided me with a diversion; taking me out of myself. As I listened, devoid of distractions, one song in particular made me realise there was no decision to make there was only one answer for Bill.

Chapter 27

After about an hour and refreshed from his siesta, Bill joined me bringing two glasses of lemonade with him.

"Good walk this morning?" he asked.

"Yes, it was. A bit hot but we managed. Lovely couple. I was thinking, when they come and pick up their hire car; maybe you could invite them here for a barbeque one evening. What do you think?"

"Sounds good to me. They're collecting a Swift this evening; I'll put it to them then." He looked into my eyes "No pressure but have you had any thoughts?"

"Yes", I replied. "That's the real reason I went to the allotment, to have time to myself and to make a list of why I should consider leaving my little house and those I have come to know and love in favour of going to live in a country I know pretty well nothing about."

Bill's face fell.

"I need to read these out to you, after which I have one more thing to tell you and then I will give you my decision."

I started with the Australia list, omitting one of the positives. Moving onto Aspros there were some negatives but it was obvious the plus points far outweighed these as well as the positives for going to Australia. When I finished, Bill stood up and started to walk back indoors.

"No wait." I told him. "I still have one more thing to tell you and then you will understand my decision."

"You don't have to say any more." his eyes filled with sadness. "Your lists say it all. You'll be staying!"

"You must let me finish." I retorted forcefully. "Please come back and sit down again. I have more to say."

"Can't imagine what." he replied sounding annoyed at my insistence.

He sat down and as he had done with me the previous night, I took his hands in mine and looked into his eyes.

"It was George Harrison who made up my mind."

"What do you mean?" Bill snapped "The guys been dead for about nine years. I suppose he appeared to you as some kind of transcendental apparition! Oh get real Polly!"

Flushed in the face, I could see he was annoyed and not thinking straight. My fault, I had not handled this at all well, I should not have read out the pros and cons and in particular not have left out the one all-important plus for Australia. I should have come straight to the point. This was the second time I had cocked things up! I held onto his hands firmly.

"I was listening to him on my MP3 player and in particular to the words of his song 'What is Life?'. It was the chorus actually and as I cannot sing you will have to put up with me just saying it." I held his hands tighter and recited, "*Tell me, what is my life without your love? Tell me, who am I without you, by my side?* The answer is 'nothing' Bill. I know I have made the most dreadful bodge of telling you but, I want to come and live in Australia with you. I am nothing without you Bill."

And then I starting blubbing and through my sobs I spouted.

"We are meant to be together. I love you and I want to come to Australia with you. I know I live here on my own six months of the year and even though we can now Skype I miss you terribly during those six months; I can't stay here forever without you."

We sat there momentarily in silence. I waited for his reaction.

"Christ! I really thought you were going stay, I thought this was going to be the end of us. I was going inside to pack my bags."

He stood up, pulled me to my feet, hugged me tightly to him till I could hardly breathe and whispered in my ear,

"I don't know what to say." But he managed. "I want to go and tell everyone." He beamed adding "I meant what I said about if you don't like Oz. It's nothing like Aspros."

Grace and Mark leapt at the barbeque invite and we agreed on Monday evening. They arrived smiling, clasping two bottles, one of wine and the other ouzo. Grace was quite upset when we told them this was our last summer on the island.

"When we get home, Mark and I were going to book for May next year and I guess we kind of assumed you would be here. We were planning on coming on some of your walks Polly."

I smiled, "Ah well, you have George Harrison to blame for that."

They looked at me questioningly. It was Bill who replied.

"Probably best left unexplained." and then looking up to the skies he added. "But I sure have a lot to thank him for."

We both laughed and to change the subject I told them they must come back, after all Stavros may rent my house as a holiday home. Grace smiled,

"That would be perfect."

With that she picked up her glass of wine and made a toast,

"To Polly and Bill, may you both be happy in Australia and never forget your years here on Aspros."

Bill and I looked at each other and said in unison.

"We'll drink to that!"

Word soon spread round the village. Everyone said how happy they were for us but how they would miss us too. When I told Eva she was quite upset; we both shed a few tears. No, that is a gross underestimation; we sobbed in each other's arms. When we had calmed down, wiped our eyes and blown our noses, Eva smiled and went over to a chest of drawers, pulled out the bottom drawer and took out a tablecloth.

"I embroidered this for you." she said as she handed the cloth to me.

I was deeply touched and opened it out over her table. It was square and round the edge in blue was the Greek key pattern. In the centre was a butterfly.

"This is you." she said pointing to the butterfly. "Like the butterflies that flutter from flower to flower, you are a free spirit Polly. I made this for you for your name day but please take it now."

Another tear rolled down her cheek as I kissed her.

Apart from applying for a visa, daily life carried on as normal through the rest of July and August and it was not until September that I gave leaving Aspros any serious thought. It was difficult when I started to sort through the cupboards and drawers deciding what to take, feeding Ari at Eva's (she said she was only to delighted to have him when I left), seeking a new tenant for the allotment and finding new homes for my chickens. The time when I would leave with Bill was now on the near horizon. Bill saw my sadness,

"Why don't you keep the house on until next spring? That way you are not burning all your bridges and if you really hate it in Australia, you will have the option of coming back and picking up virtually where you left off."

I told him not to be so silly. There was no question of my coming back. Having made the decision to go to Australia I knew there was no way I wanted our relationship to continue as it had. I told him I wanted to be with him for always and to wake up beside him every morning not just for six months of the year. However, there was some merit in Bill's suggestion about keeping on the house until spring; it would give Stavros the whole of the winter to look for a new tenant. I told Stavros I wanted to continue paying the rent so if things did not work out, the house was there for me as a bolt hole. Yes, keeping a bolt hole was a lie but given the current economy Stavros did not argue and was only too happy to accept my proposal.

By the beginning of October, I was in a daze and it was Bill who organised a party for our friends. Rather than upset any of the taverna owners, he arranged to hold it on the beach and asked each taverna to provide a plate or dish of their speciality which we paid them for. The wine was sourced from the shop in the village and the ouzo from the tourist supermarket. We hired the musicians that played during season at the Blue Sea plus, anyone who could play an instrument brought theirs with them. The party started in the late afternoon and ran on into the hours of darkness. As well as eating and drinking there was much laughter, dancing and, singing. The children played and ran about until exhausted, they fell asleep on the sands. When the sun set, those that felt the effects of the drop in temperature searched for drift wood and built fires to sit round. It was as if nobody in the village wanted the night to end. As Zorba said, it was 'splendiferous'!

But end it did and two days later we left Aspros.

I shut the door of my house for the last time, walked down the garden path to where Eva was waiting by the garden gate. I kissed her goodbye before climbing in the back of Yiannis's 4x4. As we drove down the dirt track I looked out of the rear window and watched Eva waving. It was more than I could bear. For Bill's sake, I so wanted to be under control but instead I howled. I thought my heart was going to come up through my throat. All I could do was hold Bill's hand and splutter through my tears.
"I'm all right."

I remember very little of the journey to the ferry but by the time we reached the port of Gemara I had cried myself out. I took myself off to the nearest bar and went straight to the loos – I looked a total fright. I splashed copious amount of cold water on my face to try to reduce the red and puffiness round my eyes. Taking several deep breaths I emerged to find the three very concerned faces of Bill, Anna and Yiannis, waiting for me at the bar.

"I'm fine. Sorry to have made such a fool of myself."

"Don't be." replied Anna "It's never good to bottle things up; it has to come out at some time, in some form or another."

After a final ouzo, Anna & Yiannis said farewell before driving back home and Bill and I walked hand in hand up the gangway and onto the ferry. I was pleased nobody was there to wave us off. Instead we stood side by side, hand in hand as the ferry pulled away from the harbour until gradually Aspros fell from view.

Chapter 28

I have been living in Australia for nearly three years now. Bill's house was not at all how I imagined it would be. There was no brashness or sterility in its construction. It was almost as though it had grown up through the ground along with its first floor balcony where we sit and look towards Smokey Cap Mountain. It oozes the warmth of a true home and I love living here and tending the garden.

Bill is gradually buying into a car sales business which he will eventually take over when the current owner retires. At that point I hope to be able to help with the accounts and general administration. We are both in our forties now and need to think of our financial future, so the business and my savings should take care of this. I stay away from the large towns and cities; I want none of these. We have everything we need here, so there is no need to venture into the hubbub. Bill's parents often pop over, I think they found me a little strange at first and I am sure they wondered what Bill had brought back with him. But now when they hug and kiss me goodbye, I can tell they are at ease with me; this strange brown skinned English woman. There is a strong social life here and I get on well with Bill's friends and have made quite a few of my own. I missed feline company so we adopted two cats named Leo and Libra after signs in the Zodiac. Leo is ginger and like Bill he is strong like the lion. Libra is white and black; she is like me, the scales; a bit up and down and indecisive!

Anna sends me emails with photographs attached, though not in the summer months of course, keeping me up to date with the family and what goes on in the village. Both Despina and Eva prefer to send letters with their news and versions on village life. Both write in Greek and translating their contents, with references to the dictionary, helps me maintain my grasp of the language.

Eva addresses me affectionately as 'παιδί μου', 'my child' and often sends me new recipes to try. If I make grammatical errors in my letters she will always correct these mistakes when she replies. Stavros is now renting my house, or I should say Maria's house, as a holiday let through an English company that specialises in traditional properties. I heard through Anna that Grace and Mark have been renting it twice a year; a fortnight in May and another two weeks towards the end of September. I read the emails and letters out to Bill; sometimes they make me quite emotional.

BUT.....

I have a new life now, here in Australia with Bill. As difficult as it was; leaving Aspros was the right decision. Those eight years, living on a small Greek island, took me out of my old self and made me realise there is more to life than money and material goods and certainly more than working all the hours imaginable to achieve these. I now have new life values. I never want to be my 'old self' again and when I feel Bill's arms around me as we lay in bed, I have no fears of ever being 'on the verge' again. As sloppy as it may sound, I know that as long as I am with Bill, I will be happy and content.

And so I have finished my book, a compilation of my diaries. The next step is to get it printed and published. This is more for self–gratification than any ideas of it becoming a best seller but I hope those who do read it will see you can take control of your life and if you so desire; change it. For me the change was without a doubt – FOR THE BETTER.

January 2014

We were woken this morning by the telephone ringing. Bill picked up the phone, he did not say a lot but I knew instinctively whatever it was; it was not good news. When he put the phone down he told me; it was Nikos, one of Bill's Greek friends who lives in Australia with his wife and children. There has been an earthquake on Aspros and that was about the extent of the news. There was no information as to whether the whole or parts of the island have been affected and there appears to be no communications. Certainly Nikos had been unable to contact his family. I was and still am; distraught. I am so worried about Eva and of course all my friends in Lionas. After trying to phone Yiannis but with no success, Bill has decided the only thing to do is to drop everything and book flights to Athens. From here we will get an onward ferry to the island. Bill has spent most of the morning on the phone, organising things at work, booking the flight and contacting his parents who will look after Leo and Libra in our absence. I have packed a couple of bags with essentials, retrieved our passports from the box file, emptied the fridge, stocked up on cat food and showered ready for the journey. I am now sitting at the bottom of the stairs ready to go. The only other thing I have done, to fill in the time, was to write these additional words at the end of the compilation of my diaries.

We have no idea what we will find when we get to Aspros but I am desperate to be there. I really wish 'Scottie' was here to beam us over! It may seem a bit over reactive to be travelling to the island but in the circumstances it is the only way we can find out for sure how things are and see if we can help in anyway. Primarily, I need to find Eva. She is well into her seventies now and I know from her letters that she has some health issues and is no longer nimble on her feet. I can't bear to think of her trapped under a pile of rubble. It's all just too awful.

I am starting to ramble and will work myself into a worse state, than I am already in, if I speculate further as to what has happened to everyone. I will stop now, go and make a fuss of the cats and wait for Bill to finish finalising our travel arrangements. Keep your fingers crossed for me; that devastation will not be as widespread as it was after the last earthquake and that everyone is still alive.

November 2014

I knew Polly had finally completed writing up her diaries. She was going to give them to me to read after she had printed and reread them herself. The printed pages that made up her book were slotted into a folder and have sat in a drawer for the past nine months. Yesterday evening I took them out and I have just finished reading them. There is a great debate in my mind, whether I should keep them for myself but I know in my heart I must honour Polly's wishes and publish them. First I need to add a few paragraphs.

After the lengthy journey from Australia during which Polly said only a few words, we arrived on Aspros. We found houses reduced to piles of rubble, others had massive cracks, roads had fallen into ravines and we could see from people's faces; there was a general sense of confusion. From Gemara we managed to get a lift and were dropped off on the main road where the turning goes down to Lionas. We were numbed by what we saw. Our first stop was at Despina's and Stavros's where a crack had rendered the shop in two. The house had fared better and we found the two of them salvaging what they could from the shop. It was a similar story as we continued walking to the junction, where Georgios's taverna had been reduced to a pile of rubble. Polly gasped at the sight, dropped her bag and took off down the dirt track at a run. I grabbed her bag and followed. We stopped briefly at Maria's house; it was virtually intact.

It was a different story further on. The walls of Eva's house were cracked but still standing but there was considerable damage to the roof. Broken roof tiles lay on the ground along with chunks of plaster from the walls. Eva sat outside with Elpida, both looked so sad and forlorn. Polly ran and threw her arms round Eva. It was all very emotional. Once they had composed themselves,

Polly asked Eva what was to be done. Eva was very confused but told Polly she had been sleeping in Maria's house but had heeded Elpida's advice and had not been inside the remains of her home to retrieve her belongings. There was one item Eva prized above all others and that was the crucifix on the wall in the living room. Both Polly and Eva had spent time kneeling in front of the cross in prayer. One thing that Polly omitted from her diaries and I am sure she would not object to me adding is; that during her time on the island Polly had followed the Greek Orthodox religion. Despite Eva's and Elpida's protestations, Polly decided to go inside. She wanted to see if she could find the cross and also assess what could be reclaimed and moved to Maria's house. I told her not to and that we should wait until the structural damage had been assessed. Polly was adamant and told me this was Greece and we may have to wait weeks for an assessment. She pushed open the door and disappeared inside. We heard her call,

"I can see it. I think I can reach it if I scramble over this collapsed wall. Yes I am sure I can get it."

Eva and Elpida crossed themselves and I called back,

"For God's sake be careful! Don't do anything rash!"

With that I had this funny sick feeling you get when there is an earth tremor and almost immediately the island rocked with an aftershock. Eva and Elpida clung to each other and we all swayed as an outside wall crumbled and more of the roof fell in. All was silent. We called but Polly did not emerge.

I found her crushed under a roof rafter. She was still with us and as I bent over I saw blood trickling from her nose and the corner of her mouth. I wiped the blood away and stroked her face and gently kissed her lips. I was vaguely aware of the sound of bells as the goats started moving about again on the land at the back of the house and of Eva scrambling over the rubble to reach us. Polly took one last look into my eyes. A tear rolled down her cheek. She opened her mouth as if to say something. She smiled and then she was gone. Eva had joined me and was just about to start a wailing lament when I told her Polly could still hear her. We both told her we loved her; I closed her eyes and kissed her one last time before we left the house to vent our sorrow.

I know Polly was happy in Australia but I also knew that a part of her remained on Aspros. Sometimes when she was sat deep in thought a smile came over her face and she would say do you remember on Aspros when..........? It was only right therefore that Eva and I should bury her in the village churchyard. I know Eva will tend and look after her grave.

To have finally found my soul mate, lover and best friend in Polly; only to lose her after a few short years, has hurt more than I am prepared to describe here. During our time together, I learnt so much more about Polly, than her diaries have shown. A seemingly hard headed prosperous business woman, Polly was proving; that despite the disappointments of her childhood, she could be successful. The other part that Polly concealed was her real self; in reality she was as fragile as a butterfly. Eva knew this; that was why she had chosen to embroider a butterfly in the centre of the tablecloth she gave her. Things in Polly's past still troubled her but so long as I kept her life as simple as possible and never pushed her into anything she was not comfortable with, I knew she need never be 'on the verge' again.

As for being 'on the verge', I have often wondered as to how accurate her doctor's diagnosis really was. Was it a ploy on her behalf to make Polly take a break from her hectic humdrum life? If she had purely prescribed a holiday, I doubt if Polly would have taken the advice. Maybe it was the threat of something serious that Polly needed before she would heed the advice. Of course, I will never know the answer.

In her will, Polly made provisions for Amy's three children but the bulk she left to me. There was a note tucked inside which asked me, should Eva outlive her, to look after her financially and make sure she never wanted for anything and when Eva had passed away to use the rest of the money to provide for my old age. I knew, even if it was possible to rebuild it, Eva would not want to live in her house again. I knew she would want to leave it as a shrine to Polly and as such it has been left in ruins. I negotiated with Stavros and I've rented Maria's house for Eva to live in for the rest of her days. Anna and Despina keep an eye on her and know they only have to ask whenever they feel she is in need. I am thankful Eva is not too proud to accept help.

I will return to Aspros when Polly's bones are white and together with Eva we will transfer them to the ossuary. Going back will be the hardest thing I will have to do in my life. Moving her bones will be bad enough but worse will be being in the village, imagining her smiling as she walked up the road in her shorts, t-shirt and walking boots and remembering us, sat on her veranda with her holding my hands and saying:-

Tell me, what is my life without your love?
Tell me, who am I without you, by my side?

Bill
November 2014

33134196R00107

Printed in Great Britain
by Amazon